A Seed in the Sun

AIDA SALAZAR

DIAL BOOKS FOR YOUNG READERS

DIAL BOOKS FOR YOUNG READERS
An imprint of Penguin Random House LLC, New York

First published in the United States of America by Dial Books for Young Readers,
an imprint of Penguin Random House LLC, 2022

Visit us online at penguinrandomhouse.com.

Library of Congress Cataloging-in-Publication Data
Names: Salazar, Aida, author. | Title: A seed in the sun / Aida Salazar. | Description:
New York : Dial Books for Young Readers, 2022. | Audience: Ages 8–12. | Audience: Grades 4–6.
| Summary: Lula, a farm-working girl with big dreams, meets Dolores Huerta, Larry Itliong,
and other labor rights activists and joins the 1965 protest for workers' rights. | Identifiers:
LCCN 2022032314 (print)| LCCN 2022032315 (ebook) | ISBN 9780593406601 (hardcover) |
ISBN 9780593406618 (ebook) | Subjects: LCSH: Grape Strike, Calif., 1965–1970—Juvenile
fiction. | CYAC: Novels in verse. | Grape Strike, Calif., 1965–1970—Fiction. | Agricultural
laborers—Fiction. | Strikes and lockouts—Fiction. | Mexican Americans—Fiction. | LCGFT:
Novels in verse. Classification: LCC PZ7.5.S23 Se 2022 (print) | LCC PZ7.5.S23 (ebook) | DDC
[Fic]—dc23 LC record available at https://lccn.loc.gov/2022032314LC | ebook record avail-
able at https://lccn.loc.gov/2022032315

Printed in the United States of America

ISBN 9780593406601

1st Printing
LSCH

Design by Jason Henry
Text set in Aptifer Slab and Tomarik

For the known and unknown farmworkers,
essential workers, and freedom fighters—
your seeds for justice will bloom.

SEMILLA

They tried to bury us
but they didn't know
we were seeds.
−Mexican Proverb

REMOLINO

I sometimes think about how
    I lost my voice.

I could have buried it in the earth,
        in the surco, the long row of dry dirt
where we planted onion bulbs last spring
while the heat of a too-hot California day
    fell on our
        arched
            backs
      like barrels
  of sun.

It could have happened
when Papá screamed for me to work faster
  just as I was singing along
    to Mamá's song
      louder than Papá's angry words
        or the drone of planes spraying the fields
          overhead.

It could have been taken
    by the roaring remolino
      that slammed into us
    like the storm of Papá's belt when we upset him,
an out of nowhere tornado
      ripping through the fields.

maybe that's when the dirt-drenched air
                                pulled
                    my voice out of my breath
          and caught it in the
                            spin of wild wind.

What's left is a whispery rasp
an orange-yellow mist
          that comes and goes
                    like clouds.

My real voice is either somewhere
          in the tumble of dirt
                    in the onion fields
          of the Imperial Valley
   or
was taken by
                    the anger of the wind.

One day, I pray it comes back.

OPEN-SKY HAMMOCKS

We drown bedbugs
in a pail of water,
chinches we pluck
>from the mattresses
propped up outside
on rusty barrack walls.

The worst kind of chore
on our first day in Delano,
in another labor camp
as terrible as the last
and the one before that.

Concha and Rafa race to see
who can drown more bugs.
They beat me by a lot
because they're
five and four years older.

I ask Mamá if we can sleep
in our hammocks instead
but she doesn't turn around.
She still can't hear the tiny hiss
that comes from me when I try to speak.

"¡Mamá!" I try to say louder.

She reads the question on my lips.

"Lula, the mattresses are better so we are together
and not hanging like leaves from the trees."

Me? I'd rather sleep outside
in a crest of oaks
        at the edge of the grape fields
        all around us
        with surcos like long fingers
        spread throughout the vineyard
        and thick vines
        growing big across the wires.

I'd rather sleep beneath
        a blue-black sky glistening
        with bright stars.

        A stage. A place to dream.

Where I can announce
a make-believe circus like a ringmaster
        to an audience of hooting owls
        hunting field mice in the night.

Outside under the dense, starry sky
we can only see in the back roads of California
        where we work and chase the harvests,
        so different from the city where we hardly go
        and where the glow of lights washes away the contrast.

Yes, it's colder in our hammocks
than in the one-room wooden barrack,
        especially in the winter,
        but so much better
        than getting eaten alive by chinches.

"Pero, Mamá, I wish we could . . ." I try to argue.

"No time for wishing now, Lula."

Mamá leans on my shoulder
as she passes me holding a grass broom.
Her long thick braid lays against her neck
as her body bends like a willow branch,
and she sighs,

"Vamos, Lula, Concha, Rafa. Let's keep cleaning,
mis amores."

LIGHT BLUE SCHOOLHOUSE

I watch water glisten as it splashes
      against the tin of the pail I fill
at the only tap at this new but familiar camp.
      I think of the light blue schoolhouse
      I saw from the truck as we arrived,
           and my panza flutters.

I wonder about the new school year
and if the school will have
a twelfth grade for Concha
and a seventh grade for me
because there's never a guarantee.

A school!
Where we'll be the new faces
along with other farmworker kids
whose families came like ours
for the grape harvest
and who also won't know
what they'll be learning
and will struggle to catch up.

An actual school!
Not housework,
not watching my baby siblings,
and not field work.

Back in Bakersfield
Rafa missed so many days
he was whittled down two whole grades.
      That's when he had it

and instead followed Papá and Mamá
into the fields each daybreak
to pick whichever crop was in season.
Truant officers didn't even blink
to see him in the fields
as dandelion tall as he is.

I'd taken what Concha
once told me to heart.
No matter how much we miss,
no matter if teachers are mean,
no matter they sometimes punish us
for speaking Spanish,
no matter if we can't keep friends,
school is ours.

"Lula, you're here to soak up anything you can,
porque tomorrow, we'll be on the road again
and the only thing you can take with you"
—she tapped my head— "is up here."

The best thing about Concha
is she loves school
as much as me.
Concha's gentle brown eyes
are maps
when I can't find my way.

BABY WORK

Papá comes back
with work orders from the crew leader
and a face folded in worry.

He, Mamá, and Rafa
will pick grapes tomorrow morning.
    Our baby sister, Gabriela,
    and babiest brother, Martín,
    will go with them
so Concha and I can get to school.

Mamá doesn't ask us to
work the fields to pick cotton,
potatoes, strawberries, or grapes
because that's when school's in session.

Mamá doesn't ask us to skip school
to watch the babies, either,
she likes what we learn
about the world outside the fields.
She loves to hear us translate for her
the stories in the books we get to read,
the English transforming into the Spanish
that she and Papà speak.

Threat of a truant officer
or no truant officer,
I don't think Mamá
would want it any other way.

I wouldn't mind watching the babies,
Gabi and Martín are
two balls of sweet masa with legs.

Gabi's almost three and runs
like a cheetah on her bare feet
with one too many toes on each foot.
Mamá calls her "una hija de Dios"
and because she's a child of God,
she is perfect just as she is
with no need for shoes
we can't afford anyway.

Martín crawls like a ladybug
because being one year old is still pretty little.
         He reaches up
         with his
         dimpled hands
         whenever he wants
         to be carried,
and we always happily sweep him up.

It's not hard to do squishy baby work like that.

ESCABS

I overhear Papá tell Rafa,

> "Caramba, we just walked into a strike. Men with picket
> signs and bullhorns were yelling at all of us not to
> work."

> "What do you think they're fighting for, Apá?"

I get closer but he pulls Rafa inside,
and gives me a "what do you want, nosy"
kind of look but I can still hear him.

> "Los Filipinos seem to have left the fields because they
> want higher wages. They're en huelga, and they think
> we're taking their jobs," he says.

> "Do you think there'll be trouble, Apá?" Rafa asks.

> "Pues they were protesting and screaming 'Don't
> be escabs!' at us while we were getting crew orders.
> Josesito said *escab* means traitor because we are crossing
> their picket line."

Papá says the word *scab* like
his tongue is a skipped record
adding a syllable up front.

Mamá is sitting on the edge of the bed,
holding her head between her hands
like she's hurt,
frowning into her closed eyes.

I want to see what's wrong with her
but I stay outside the barrack
so Papá doesn't know
I'm snooping.

Martín toddles up to Papá,
reaches up to him.
Papá unfolds his brows and arms,
lifts him up and tosses him into
the air with an "Ah, ¡mi muchachito!"

Papá saves his sweetness for the babies.
As soon as we get older,
seeing his love for us
is a sight as rare as rain
falling on desert earth.

CARPA SMILES

I remember a time
before the whirlwind,
a time before Gabi and Martín were born
when we snuck into the circus.
Rafa and me.

Papá went without
his bottles of beer for once
to buy three tickets
for Mamá, Concha, and him.

Hidden behind crates,
Rafa held up the tent's wall
to keep me from getting scratched
like he did as he crawled
beneath the canvas.

We emerged into a flurry of people
trying to get a seat to see La Carpa Vázquez,
the traveling Mexican circus.

We squirmed, pushed, and shoved
other kids to sit up front.
As the lights began to dim,
I searched and found
Concha, Mamá, and Papá
sitting still inside a crowd
moving like ants around them.

Suddenly the lights, the music,
and a loud, booming voice
welcomed us.

"Señoras y señores, niños y niñas, welcome to the
world-famous La Carpa Vázquez!"

That's when I saw it.
Papá's smile,
     with its missing right-side molar.
        A smile so pretty and wide
          it shined like a galaxy
            in the center
         of the deep brown night
           of his face.

I don't understand why
he never lets us see it,
but seeing him smile
because of the ringmaster's smooth voice
     opened up my own sonrisa
        like a squash bloom
           following
              the light of day.

I swept my head around
     and was pulled like never before
     and never since
     into the magic of la carpa.

The clown jugglers,
        the comedians, the singers,
the dancing dog show,
     the tightrope walkers,
        and the flying trapeze.

Rafa and me clapped, hollered,
        and fell on each other,
¡muriéndonos de risa!

When I took a breath,
        a dream was etched in my heart,
                to join the circus one day,
                as ringmaster.

I think about the ringmaster
whenever I am still.

I think about how his voice
made the lights of Papá's face
        come alive.

I want to be one of the reasons Papá smiles.

WILTED MAMÁ

Before the sun awakens
    and roosters begin to sing
    the next morning,
I hear a shuffling
    but it isn't Mamá
    getting breakfast ready
by the light of a lantern.
    It's Rafa and Papá
    stumbling and grumbling.

I lift my head to see
    Mamá sleeping,
Gabi and Martín like two scorpions
    clinging to her body.

I nudge Concha awake next to me
    just as Papá nearly spits
    for us to get up
    to make desayuno.

The coolness of the morning
    warms quickly
with the approaching
    late summer heat of Delano
and I step out
    to start the fire
    in the outdoor stove.

Concha follows me
    with a stack of tortillas.
    The only food we have left.

Rafa lifts his eyebrows at us
        because we've never seen Mamá
        stay in bed like this.

Mamá is stronger than mesquite.
        No torment, no weather, no drought
        could down her.
She never misses work.
        Not when she gave birth to us,
        not when our other baby brother, Ángel,
        slipped away from dysentery.
She and Papá worked for weeks
        with tears pouring
        down their faces
        along with their sweat.

Concha looks at me
        takes a deep breath,
        lays the tortillas on the comal.
She tells me I should go to school alone
        so she can stay
        to help Mamá.

I shake my head feverishly,
        my bottom lip quivers.
School without Concha?
        No. I can't do it.

        "What if they don't hear me?"

        "They'll hear you fine. Your voice is only raspy, Lula,
        not gone. Just speak up and take your time."

Her face falls away in a distant sadness.

"Do it for Mamá."

Mamá wakes then and calls out
        our names in a chain,
        "Concha, Rafa, Lula."
Papá follows us in to see her.

Mamá nods slowly
        as if she is wilted,
        and unfolds a subtle smile.
She isn't feeling well enough
        to go into the fields
        but she's strong enough to stay home
with the babies without Concha.

        "Will you be okay alone?" I ask.

        "Yes, por supuesto, mi'ja. Both of you girls go. I will
        manage with the little ones just fine."

When Concha and I
        step through the doorway,
        guilt pours over me because
I can't wait
        to get to the light blue schoolhouse.
I turn back to see Mamá sitting up,
        waving a tiny sign of the cross in our direction
        her pale face holds
        a soft and sleepy expression
        as the daytime
comes into the room.

SEEDS

Mamá once told me
about the magic of seeds.

Seeds hold power in their tiny bodies.
Each grain, each kernel, each bulb
is a miracle of life.

If given the right soil,
        enough water,
                enough light,
                        though buried,
                                a seed will rise
                                        with its growing limbs
                                                to touch the sun.

Mamá said
seeds hold the memory of others
that came before them,
a destiny to become something else
        larger, greater, and richer
        than they once were.

They are meant to give new seeds,
        carrying their miracle inside
                from beginning to end.

"Like you, mi Lulita, and all of God's children on Earth," Mamá said.

TO SCHOOL

We walk a path of
     wild grasses,
     wild sunflowers,
     weeds and seeds
to school.

Concha throws her arms   into the air
     and dreams out loud.

     "When I get to college there will be no stopping me."

The skin of her cheeks is kissed by the morning sun.

     "Stopping you from what?" I ask.

     "From getting us away from field work. Away from all of
     this! See, after college, I can get a fancy job in a big city
     somewhere and support us."

     "But then you'll come back, right?" I ask, afraid of
     the answer.

Concha laughs,
scoops me up from behind,
     and twirls me around, laughing,
          unbothered that she might mess up her blouse
     or that my too-big shoes
will flop off my feet,

     "Of course, silly!"

I squint my eyes at the horizon
as I hear a ruckus in the distance.
People have bullhorns, are shouting,
they sound excited, maybe angry.

I point out
                a red flag
                draped from a pickup truck.
It has a white circle
        in the center
                    and inside the circle
                        is a black silhouette of a bird.
                    Is it an eagle?
Concha reads the letters
        sprawled on top,

        "NFWA" and another sign, "AWOC AFL-CIO."

It's all a broken puzzle
we don't understand.

Worry burrows
into my head.

I want to ask Concha
if this means trouble for our family
because of what I overheard from Papá.

But I can't form the question
and keep walking
with my unknowingness
toward school.

LEONOR

The pretty blue schoolhouse
is a trick of the mind
        because when you get up close
        it's as junked out and rusted
        as an abandoned Chevy.
But I don't care because
I think I made a friend.

Leonor is in my grade,
a fast talker with a slight lisp.
She leaves almost no room
for the thin words
        dangling
        from my mouth.
I'm relieved to sit back and listen.

Leonor is Filipina and Mexican,
and her dad works here year-round,
which is sort of lucky because
        she doesn't have to up and move
        to follow the crops like us
though unlucky because
        she lives in the chinche barracks too.

She knows everyone at school
and if she doesn't
she introduces herself
like she did with me.

  "It's probably hard coming to a new school," she says,
  "so I try to make it easy. Besides, I like to memorize names!"

At lunch, she tests her memory
by pointing at the kids
and saying where they are from
as they move across the yard.

She names
        Filipino kids from Stockton
        Mexican kids from Arizona
        Negro kids from Texas
        Puerto Rican kids from Hawaii
        Arab kids from Michigan
        and Oakie kids from Idaho.[1]

A few I know because
we follow the California fields together,
but my shyness holds me back.

The wobble of my voice
straightens out with Leonor
when I get a few words in
to answer where I'm from.

        "I'm Mexican but born in Salinas."

She is sweet,
though she scrunches her face at me
when she can't make out what I say
as if that will help her hear me.

---

1   See author's note.

CHISME ENGINE

At the end of lunchtime
    a crowd of kids
        surround Leonor
    like she's a conductor
calling everyone aboard.

    They're talking about the strike,
    and it feels like chisme
    not everyone's supposed to know.

I come close enough to listen
to Leonor fit another piece
of the strike puzzle into place.

    "My tito Larry started this strike just last week with
    other Filipino workers. They're forcing the growers to
    pay them better."

A curly-haired Arab boy
I've never seen speaks up,

    "That's their business, not ours. My dad came to do
    the work they don't want to do."

Leonor is quick,

    "Yeah, if you are new, it probably means your family is
    strikebreaking. Pass it on! Convince your dad to join
    the strike, that way my titos will get paid
    better and so will he."

The boy argues,

"Those growers are too big and rich! They'll never
pay the workers more."

Leonor is a locomotive
whose engine revs
as she holds her
fists at her hips
and says,

"Oh yeah, my titos already won a strike in Coachella
earlier this year. Whatcha gotta say about that, Mohamed?"

I stare at Leonor.
I've never seen a strike before
though I think I did hear
about the one in Coachella.
I love to watch her take control,
moving us all with
her fast-engine tongue.

MI VOZ

I try not to sink
        into the sadness
I feel to not have
        a voice like Leonor's.

I still don't know when mine will return.

Concha says it's like "laryngitis"
        that's stuck around
        for more than a year.

It embarrasses me
        for others to hear
                its thin sound,
so I speak only when I have to.

I wonder if my voice
        will change   when puberty comes
like Rafa's did.

Concha says it's starting to happen.
She can tell by the pimples
        popping up
                across my forehead
and how my cheeks have lost
                their baby chub.

I wonder if puberty
        will also give me the courage
to speak up like Leonor
        even if my laryngitis
never goes away.

BEATING CRIES

When we get home
    a pot of beans
        is boiling over
            on the outdoor stove.

We find Mama drenched in sweat,
    shifting in her sleep.
Her face, red with blemishes.
Her rosary beads, wound lightly
around the cradle of her hand.

Gabi and Martín are on the ground,
playing with a green beetle
    and the smell of vomit
        rises from a bedpan on the floor
near the head of the bed.

Gabi comes to me
    and Concha grabs Martín.
We pat their backs
    as they whimper.

They don't have full sentences
    to tell us what they've seen.
    Why Mamá is still in bed.

Concha gently nudges Mamá's shoulder.

    "We're home from school, Mamita," she says.

Mamá mumbles and stirs.
　　　Her eyes move restlessly
　　　　　　behind her closed lids.

　　　I try, "Mamá. It's me, Lula."

I touch Mamá's forehead
　　　like she does to us
　　　when we aren't well.
The back of my hand
　　　remains hot
　　　when I remove it
from her feverish skin.

　　　"What do we do, Concha?"

　　　"I don't know," she says softly.

She leaves the room
with a loaded bedpan
in one hand
　　　and Martín
　　　straddled on her hip.

That's an answer
Concha has never given me.
She's always known.
　　　Everything.

I hug Gabi tightly.
　　　She buries her crying little face
　　　into my shoulder.
Fear beats hard
inside my chest
until I cry too.

WHEN THE SUN COMES DOWN

I hear a soft roar of sounds.

        Talking,   laughter,

     trucks arriving,   people walking.

I stand at the doorway

       see Papá and Rafa at the far end

       of the row of barracks

       coming home with other farmworkers.

They are baked and dusty

       tumbleweeds,

          their clothes dirty,

    with big wet sweat patterns

circling their backs and armpits.

Scared rushes of blood rise

     from my heart

     to my throat.

I place Gabi on the ground

       and rush to them for help.

Papá looks down at me with surprise.

     "¿Qué te pasa, Lula? What's got into you?"

I want to tell him to hurry

     because

Mamá looks really sick

     and

Concha doesn't know what to do

     but

the stampeding beats of my heart

tear.
at.
my.
breath.

I grunt. A small, fragile, wordless punch.

I pull Papá's arm. "¡Ven!" I want to say
       but
instead I point to our barrack.

         "Muchacha terca, speak, for heaven's sake." He barks
         and pulls his arm away from my grip.

         "Ma . . . má!" finally seeps out of me in fear-filled syllables.

Papá stops suddenly,
looks at my tormented face,
          turns over to Rafa,
          and they both take off running
toward our barrack.

         "Vieja. Viejita, ¿qué te pasa?" Papá shakes her.

The rest of us are a flock of doves
crowded around Mamá and Papá.
         Mamá opens her eyes slightly.
She looks at Papá for a second
before her eyes roll back
into her head.

Papá swiftly lifts her
into his arms
like a rag doll.

He doesn't look scared
but determined
like he does
when clearing a mess of weeds.

"¡Abran camino!" he shouts at us.

I tremble as we step back to let him pass.

"Where are you taking her, Papá?" Rafa asks.

"I'm going to ask Josesito to drive us to a doctor."

Rafa stumbles
as he hurries
behind him.

Papá doesn't look back to see
         how the rest of his children
         hold one another,

         how our tears stream down
         our frightened faces,

         how we are broken as branches
         fallen from a lightning-struck tree.

GERMEN

Deeds and seeds,
take their own time to fructify.
—Mahatma Gandhi

LUCRECIA

Mamá named me Lucrecia,
an old name she borrowed
from her grandmother
who raised her.

Mamá's parents
died when she was little
and she didn't have siblings,
so Abuelita Lula
was Mamá's only family.

Mamá says when she was
pregnant with me,
though her grandmother
was gone too, she felt
Abuelita's presence when
the sun broke open
each morning.

Mamá saw it as a sign
to give me, the baby
swimming in her body,
Abuelita Lula's name
because Lucrecia
means light.

AT DAY'S END

The Delano heat begins to soften.
It's been hours since they've gone.

Concha and I put the babies to bed,
still afraid as we wait on wooden crates

staring out into the late-night movement
of the camp through our open door.

I watch the lanterns from
each of the shacks turn out

one by one until the theater of stars
begins to glow above the tin roofs.

I daydream onto a stage
            wearing a long red coat
            and button-down shirt
            tall black boots and a top hat
            as I announce—

I am stopped by two lights
that come with an approaching car.

We crowd Josesito's car as it stops
in front of our barrack,

ignoring the cloud of dirt
it's kicked up.

I hold my breath with a wish
for Mamá to be okay.

CURACIÓN

Mamá's weak head
    is a swooning ship.

Papá tells us the emergency room wouldn't see her
unless he had one hundred dollars.
    He lays her on my parents' bed,
    walks out, his jaw clenched,
        pulling a half-gone bottle of vodka
        from his empty back pocket.

Rafa gathers the basket of questions
we offer and gives us answers.

    On the outskirts of town,
    they found a curandera
    who attends to those
        cursed with mal de ojo
        by jealous neighbors,
        shriveling up from too much heat,
        or poisoned, like Mamá,
        in the fields.

Poisoned?

Doña Serafina suspects
Mamá has been hurt by pesticides
    the crop dusters in the fields spray.

I immediately regret sometimes thinking
    the droplets that fall
    from those planes

against the light
on the green fields
were ever beautiful.

I recall the stench of chemicals
        left behind on our clothes
though we wash it off
in the irrigation canals
        from where we also drink.

Rafa says that Doña Serafina
gave Mamá an herbal tonic,
        laid her on a petate on the ground,
                where Mamá vomited a dark tar into a basin,
                until she was empty
                of lo malo
                and limp
                with sleep.

A WELL OF VODKA

Papá stares at us
from the doorway.
    A well of frustration in his eyes
    so deep it drowns
my courage to speak.

    He says, "No more school for you, Concha. We need your
    wages in el fiel. Y tú, Lula, will stay home to take care
    of your mother."

Concha's voice quivers when she objects,

    "I can't leave now; this is the time to apply for college."

Concha dives headfirst
into the deepening flood
building in Papá.

For him, college is for
the children of rich ranch owners
and not for migrant farmworkers or girls like us.
    We are not meant for la universidad.

    "Papá, it'll give me a chance for a better job and maybe
    you wouldn't have to work so hard. We'd have money
    for more food than just beans and tortillas, and maybe
    we would've had money to pay for a doctor for Mamá."

Papá's face twists
    with humiliation.

I know Concha   didn't mean   to offend him,
to say that he   could not   provide for his family
      or worse,
that Mamá   not getting   a doctor's help
      was his fault,
but her words   split open   something in Papá.

     "I am a man who works hard!" Papá says, slurring into
     his drunk words.

He trips   as he lunges   for Concha.
     She pulls back.
He sways   and catches himself
     on a table nearby.

     "I may not have money for doctors but I am an
     honest man with too many mouths to feed!"

Rafa stands in front of him
but Papá   pushes Rafa away   with the force of a bull.

Papá lifts his arm high
in front of Concha and
     slaps her to the ground
with his calloused hand.

     "From now on, everybody will earn their keep and those
     that can't,"—Papá points at Gabi and Martín asleep on
     the bed near our sick Mamá,—"will have to fend for
     themselves!"

I rush to wrap my arms around Concha.

Papá is
     a raging river of alcohol
          who's burst open its dam.

A FLOWER HEART

Before I fall asleep
Concha cries so quietly
she sounds like a soft whistle.

Lying next to her
I put my hand over hers
and squeeze gently.

I wonder if I should
tell Mamá when she feels better
how cruel Papá was to us?

What could she have done,
as sick as she is?
Even if she wasn't sick,
what would she have done?
Mamá has often stood silent
when Papá laid the belt
or the switch on our behinds.

Maybe if she were healthy,
he never would have gotten drunk
and said and done such terrible things.

Maybe seeing Mamá so sick
scared him.

Inside Papá, there is a smiling man
who sometimes wraps Mamá in a hug
who sometimes laughs,
who sometimes cries,
though it is hard to see.

Papá is a cactus plant
who lives in the harshest conditions
with a prickly shell
and a desert flower
who blooms
only once a year.

A KNOT

The next day, I'm alone
with Mamá, Gabi, and Martín.

Mamá groans awake and asks for water.
I lift her neck as she drinks.

I offer her the herbs again
just as Rafa told me to do.

Mamá gags but takes them.

    "Gracias, mi amorcito," she says, bending her tired eyes
      into half-moons.

Gabi runs in circles in the barrack
and bounces on our empty bed.

I pretend I am Mamá, not Lula,
and get to tidying up the room.

I organize our small shelf of dishes,
prepare to make atole for lunch.

Gabi runs through my legs
and almost trips me.

When I call her name
it is a hardly audible dribble.
Gabi spins in place.
She giggles.

    "Gabi!" I try again.

She rips right by and lifts off with a jump
straight toward Mamá's bed.

She falls short of the bed
and lands flat on her belly.

Her head smacks the floor
with the sound of a clap.

Mamá shoots up.

Gabi wails and holds her head
with her little hand.

Martín takes his first solo steps toward her
but falls and launches into a cry too.

Mamá reaches for Gabi
and when she moves her hand

there is a knot—the reddish purple of a ripe plum—
growing on Gabi's forehead.

    "Shhh, ya mi amor. It's okay. It's okay."

Mamá cradles her.
With a free hand, she scoops up Martín.
I crumble with guilt.

In my mind, I hear Papá say "earn your keep"
and my eyes fill with lágrimas.

    "No pasa nada, Lula. It was an accident," Mamá says,
      her face pale and puffy. "They are little and they will fall."

Mamá is forgiving
of the disaster I am.

What will Papá do
when he finds out

Gabi got hurt
because she didn't hear

my good-for-nothing
voice?

HIDDEN

Mamá and the babies nap together
      curled into one another
like a walnut in a shell.

Mamá always says,

      "Todo sana cuando uno duerme,"

so it calms me to watch her sleep
and know she is healing.

The day has been long
but I know Rafa and Concha
will be home soon
      and with them
      the storm of Papá.

Someone comes to the door
and I hurry to it before they knock.
I step outside to see Leonor,
my new friend, with a group of women
and some other kids with papers in their hands.

      "Lula! You live here? So cool! I live just over there!"
      Leonor's words pour out. "Why'd you miss school, anyway?
      You okay?" Leonor doesn't stop to hear my answer. "Hey,
      guess what. There's a house meeting
      tomorrow night for farmworkers, you should come."

A small, dark-haired woman
standing next to Leonor
looks at me with gentle eyes.

She wears a button,
the same puzzling image of the eagle
and the "NFWA" I saw on the flag.

The woman says to me in English,

>"Yes, please let your family know. It's about the
>Filipino strike. The National Farm Workers Association
>needs to decide if we want to support the work
>stoppage or not."

I nod, trying to understand.

She hands me a newspaper
about the NFWA and tells me
to give it to my parents.
She tips her head to me, smiles
and walks away to the next barrack,
grabbing for the hand
of a little girl no bigger than Gabi.

Leonor waves goodbye to me as she moves to catch up.

>"Dolores, I mean, Mrs. Huerta, wait for me!" she says to
>the woman but then yells back, "I'll see you at school
>tomorrow, Lula!"

I take the newspaper,
too afraid to say anything
to Papá right now,
>and I tuck it away
>like a squirrel
>where he can't see it
and I can read it for myself, later.

IGNITION

The ripe purple plum
popping from Gabi's forehead
gives away the truth
of the mess I made
of things today.

But it isn't the first thing Papá
notices when he walks in.

> A different Papá
> flickers before me,
> a gentler, more caring Papá
> than the one who exploded
> in flashes the night before.

> He steps lightly when he
> approaches Mamá,
> caresses her face and
> whispers a prayer,

> "Pobrecita. Que Dios me la cuide."

> Mamá is brighter now
> that she's rested,
> now that she's kept food down.

Still, he looks afraid to see her this withered.
I can tell by the way he swallows hard,
by the ever so subtle tremble in his voice.
The fear gathers in the rough wrinkles
splitting the corners of his mouth.

"Papá," Gabi says sweetly, and curls her arms around
Papá's legs.

When Papá brushes
his cracked hand
across Gabi's head,
he feels the bump
and pauses.

He bends down
and inspects her.
Gabi touches her knot,
looks at Papá and then
up at me.

"How could you let this happen, Lula?!" Papá yells.

I lower my head.

There it is again.
His rising anger
flaring like a match
struck on.

"I'm s o o o r r y, Papá."

He comes closer and speaks through gritted teeth,

"You were supposed to take care of them," he says,
forgetting that he said the babies should "fend for
themselves" when he was drunk.

"Osvaldo." Mamá calls his name. "It was an accident."

49

"What you need is to work in the fields, now that your mother is better." His eyes narrow in front of me.

"Tranquilo, Osvaldo," Mamá says again, lifts her arm as if to tell him to stop.

"No, Ramona. She's coming to work so she can learn how not to be so inútil."

He's said many mean things before
but never called me useless.

My voice drops away from me.

I back away from him slowly
afraid he'll hit me
like he did
Concha.

When I get to the door
all I can think is to
                RUN
                from
                Papá's
                fire.

RUNNING

"Lula!"

I hear Concha calling,
her footsteps trailing.

But I am swelling
with my own fire now
at what I can't do anything about,
    like Mamá being sick
      not being able to go to school
      not keeping Gabi safe
      and how far away I am
      from making Papá proud.

So I run and run.

"Lula! Wait!"

Concha follows somewhere behind me.

I open my mouth to see
if the hot wind will
         pour
     my old voice
back into
my throat
like a soothing manzanilla tea
that would heal
        all
           of
              my
                  hurt.

QUELITES

I stop at an unattended field of quelites
in whose green arms
I am safe.

Calma. Calma, Lula.
I tell myself.
Calma.

I breathe in the scent of green leaves
bent and broken beneath my feet.

I remember the day Mamá taught me
how to pick wild mustard greens
to add them to the food we cook.

She taught me to know
when they were good for eating
by noticing the width and texture
of their dark wispy leaves,
by paying close attention
to the way they sprang up in clusters
that signaled there was water nearby.

> "My abuela, en paz descanse, said the earth loves us
> by giving us what we need to survive. We just need to
> learn to see it," she said.

> "If that's true, why can't we eat everything we pick,
> Mamá?" I asked wondering about all the times we had
> gone hungry after a full day of harvesting.

"Because land has been claimed and not shared.
Though La Tierra belongs to no one. And because for
some, having enough is not enough."

Mamá said, aside from quelites,
we could forage mushrooms, berries,
and other wild things.

"We've been picking them for as long as the earth has
given them, for as long as we have needed to live."

Mamá tore the leaves
with a soft twist of her hand
and whispered something under her breath.

"Remember to ask permission and to thank her, Lula. La
Tierra knows if we are ungrateful."

The growers think quelites are weeds.
They think we are doing them a favor
by picking them from their open-wide fields
on all of the land they've claimed for themselves.

MALCRIADA, I

When Concha finds me,
      my blouse is a hammock full
of mustard greens I gathered
to cook for Mamá.

      "You really scared me, Lula! Though I don't blame you
      for running."

Concha touches the place on her cheek
      where Papá's hand landed
and plops down next to me
with a newspaper
in her hand.

She didn't find it squirreled away
      inside our bedsheets, like I thought.
It was her own copy given to her
by a woman and her children
when Concha was coming off the fields.

As I read the top
of the newspaper,
I wonder if it was the same woman
with Leonor who gave me a copy.

      "El Malcriado: The Voice of the Farmworker,"

Papá uses the word *malcriado*
      for those who are misbehaving,
and I feel the memory of Papá's angry words
want to close up my throat.

"Are the farmworkers calling themselves rascals?" I ask
    Concha.

"Nah, that's a name for kids like you who run away."
    Concha grins.

I whack her playfully
        on the arm
        and stick
                my tongue out
        at her,
widening her grin
into a laugh.

EL MALCRIADO, TOO

As we read,
      we finally unlock
the NFWA puzzle.

     The National Farm Worker's Association
     is an organized group of farmworkers.
     The red flag, white circle, and black eagle silhouette
     is their symbol like the Mexican flag's eagle
     and they've got two leaders—
     Cesar Chávez and Dolores Huerta.

     "Aha! That's got to be the same Dolores Huerta who
     gave me a newspaper!" I offer up.

     "Wait, let me read more. It says here . . ."

By the time Concha and I read
through the entire paper, we understand
     the Filipino strikers have a union
     AWOC—the Agricultural Workers Organizing Committee,
     and the Mexican workers are the NFWA.

     The AWOC are gathering
     in picket lines on the fields
     to ask those harvesting
     to join them in the strike.
It's the only way to pressure the growers,
just like Leonor said.

Then we confirm
     those who work the fields
     right now are called scabs

56

and are thought to be traitors
to the union.

"Concha, isn't that what you, Papá, and Rafa have been
doing?" I ask, remembering what the strikers called
Papá when he got his work orders.

"Híjole, that's terrible! We've got to go to that meeting
and find out more," Concha says, folding the newspaper
into her armpit and helping me up.

I get a chill to think how, tomorrow
when I go to work the fields,
I will not only be a malcriada to Papá
but a scab to the strikers too.

SACRIFICES

When we get back
we enter slowly to see
Papá observing
Mamá's progress.

Instead of using the bedpan,
Rafa has helped her
to the camp outhouses and back,
and is settling her into bed again.

Mamá's gratitude is held in the cup
of her hand lightly tapping Rafa's cheek.

"My body hurts, but I'll be okay," she says.

Mamá lifts her outstretched arm,
asking us all to come closer.

I am safe from Papá's stare.
He now sits on a wood crate nearby,
looking down at his hands
like he is in prayer
so I feel okay to do as Mamá asks.

"You are los grandes of this family. We are going to need
you more for the time being." Mamá's words are
measured and kind.

"We know, Mamá. We're here." Rafa brushes her hair
away from her face.

"My good boy," she says. She pauses to take a deep
breath before she begins again. "Yes, but I'm speaking
about your sisters because giving up school isn't easy
for them."

Concha asks Mamá not to worry.
We will never abandon her
or our family.

"Gracias, hija," Mamá says. "Your wages from working
will be the most useful. I can watch the bebés yo sola.
As soon as I feel better, you'll be able to go back to school."

Papá walks out in silence.

The loving air Mamá
breathed into the room
is cut
by
each
of
his
hard
steps.

INSIDE THE CANOPY

Before the sun awakens and appears
      at the thin seam made
by the fields and the sky,
          we climb onto the back of a pickup truck,
          an old jalopy that will take us
          further out into the vineyards.

A chorus of "buenos días" salute us.

The workers, our neighbors,
all farmworkers too
      are a sleepy but ready
      bouquet of brown faces that smile
      despite the difficult work
we all know lays ahead.

      We ride standing up like tightly
      packed cigarettes in their carton.
      The words *scab, traitor, malcriada*
      spin in my mind.

The woodsmoke of the recently used
outdoor stoves of our workers' camp
      wafts through the air
          and mixes
      with the smell of dew
and fresh dirt.

My pants and long sleeves feel
warm against my body but I know
          the Delano heat

will bake me
in its oven
and without their cover,
the sun will burn
my already darkened skin
until it hurts.

I tug   on the handkerchief   around my neck,
secure the other one
holding back my hair.

The grape vines are lush and loyal.
They stretch and twirl along the wires.
They always bear fruit.

I feel lucky I'm small,
I don't have to crouch
but can easily get underneath the canopy of vines to look
for clusters of purple
or green grapes.

My parents taught us
when the grapes were "a su punto,"
so perfectly ripe and ready for picking.
They said uvas don't ripen
after they've been picked,
so it's necessary to cut them
when they are plump and sugary sweet
and easy to pull in a cluster.
If the uvas are dark green and small,
or the vines still feathery with tiny flowers
then we need to
leave them.

I am careful not to tug too much on a stem.
If it isn't ready and I yank too hard,
I could break it and the grapes
would never sweeten.

My favorite way to know
if they are ready,
is to pick one grape,
pop it into my mouth,
and bite down.

When my teeth tear
through the skin
and the sweetness of grape juice
floods out,
I don't need to know if they are
the right color
or easy enough   to   pull.
The sweet grape
swirling
inside
my mouth
lets me know when
to pick the cluster
and lay it carefully
into the wooden gathering tub,
and then into boxes
waiting for them
between
the rows.

AVALANCHE

As I work,
my mind is an avalanche
    of boulders
        tumbling down
    a cliff.

The first boulder
    comes crashing.

        Mamá fighting to get stronger each day.

          The knot still on Gabi's head.

        The school that Concha and I are missing.

The Filipino strike. Would we join them?

        Papá and his ever-mean mood I tiptoe around.

          Then, the carpa. Where no one can
            stop me from dreaming.

I reach for a bundle of grapes,
    cut them with my hook knife,
take them into my hands.
    I look up at the Sierra Nevada mountains in the distance
    and realize they are like gigantic boulders.

I wonder,
    are they God's daydreams and worries
          gathered and piled
            into peaks?

CONCHA'S DUST

While my sister picks and packs grapes,
Concha is wrapped in as many clothes as I am.
She doesn't complain.
She blinks away the sweat
dripping into her wishful eyes.

Concha is agile and accurate.
More than me, Rafa, or Papá.
Maybe because she's older.
Maybe because Papá's aching back
slows him down.

She fills boxes of grapes
twice as fast as anyone here.
Maybe that's why Papá
is happier to have Concha working
and increasing the family's box count
than being in school.

She says everything we've learned
in all the schools we've attended
is more than surviving, it's thriving
because nobody expects it from us.

Like Papá, most people
would have us stay workers
covered in dust and then
disappear into dust.
It's no wonder she wants more.

What if Papá doesn't let her go to college?
What if she can't go because of the days she's missed?

What if the colleges don't let her in?
So many what-ifs.

My chest tightens
when I think of life without her.
        Away at college.

                Who will help me with school,
                with chores, and dinner?
                Who will remind me to be patient with Papá,
                especially when he insists
                women and men aren't the same
                and lets Rafa off from doing
                the chores he expects from us.
                Who will point out no one
                taught Papá any different.

Concha has helped us
survive Papá this long.

I know I shouldn't feel
like I'm feeling now,
scared she'll leave
and never come back.

Maybe this is what scares Papá too
but he will never admit it.

The difference between
me and Papá is
        I wish for Concha
        what she wants most
        and Papá does not.

OSVALDO ESCLAVO

Papá didn't have
a family of his own
before us.

Mamá told us once
Papá's family was so poor,
they sold him to a rich Spanish family
in Mexico when he was seven years old.

This family made him sleep
in the back corral with the animals
he was forced to care for.
They also made him run their errands,
clean their house, and sell baked goods
the mother would make, in the market
—all without pay.

He was their slave.
Instead of Osvaldo
they called him "Esclavo."
and thought that was funny.

Mamá said Papá finally ran away
from that place when he was thirteen.
One year older than I am now.
He made it all the way
to the United States
                    alone
and he's been working
the fields since then.

Maybe because Papá didn't have a family,
he doesn't know what to do
with the one he's got now
other than put us to work.

Deep down,
I know he loves us.
He showed it
when we were babies.

I wish I could make him
unbury his love for me
and for my older siblings.

I wish to see the warmth
I know is inside of him.

A STROKE OF HEAT

Around noon, the sun
 bends
 everything
 around me
with its heat.

The grape leaves
 wilt,
 sweat weighs down
 my clothes,
 dirt
 sears my toes
 through
 the hole
 in my
 shoe.

The leaves and vines
 I hold,
 blur.
I squint my eyes
 and the fields
 begin
to swirl.

 "Papá," I try to call out.

My feet wobble.
 I come down to a squat.
 It's better when I close my eyes.

Papá ignores me.

Concha squats down next to me.
          She lifts my eyelid.
I see her face come into focus
          with one eye.

          "Lula? ¿Hermanita? You okay?"

          "Uh. I'm dizz . . ." I say, my mouth cornstarch dry.

          "Ay. You need water. I'm all out. Where'd you leave your
          water, Lula?"

          "I didn't bring any," I say, upset with myself. Mamá
          always insists we bring water when working the fields.

          "How could you forget to bring water? ¡Niña!"

Another farmworker sees us.
Paquita, Mamá's friend,
offers water from her canteen.

          "Tanto sol hace daño." Paquita has the same look Mamá
          gives us when we're learning a hard lesson.

          "Gracias. It must be in the hundreds," Concha says to
          her. "Lula, drink up, you're probably getting heat stroke.
          Water is going to make you feel better."

My arms and legs shake,
          but I keep my squat
          while I drink.

          "She can have it all but you should look for more,"
          Paquita says.

69

I can see her dusty
and worn-out huaraches
when I crack open
          my eyes.

          I pull back
     my head, and
Paquita's sweet concern
     fades in and out
     of my view
as the heat smothers me
     like a heavy blanket.

PAPÁ'S WHISTLE

I don't see Papá and Rafa,
      they must have moved
                far ahead.

But I hear Papá whistle.

His whistle is enough
      to freeze us in our tracks.
His whistle means come here.
         It means where are you?
         It means stop horsing around,
         or whining, or fighting.

We answer that whistle
no matter what it means
because we know
      if that whistle is not answered
      quickly,
      then we've got the belt
      coming.

      "Estamos acá, Papá!" Concha yells.

Suddenly, I see
Papá's thin-soled boots
on the ground
near me.

INTO THE SHADE

"Get her into some shade before the mayordomo comes,"
he says to Concha.

I feel terrible I have to stop
both Concha and me from working.

"But hurry back. The more time you are gone the less
boxes we can fill."

My heart beats fast to think about
the crew leader finding us not working.
The rush lifts me to my feet.

Concha holds me up by my waist
as we walk down the long dirt row
away from Papá
between the grape vines
toward a patch of wild trees
and the irrigation canal.

"You've got this, Lula. Straight ahead," she encourages me.

When we get to the trees finally,
she helps me lay down in the shade.
I look up at the branches
against the blue sky.
They dip and swirl.
Dip and swirl.
I hear birds.
Their song slurs.

The world folds into itself
    and shrinks
        and expands
    and shrinks again.

Darkness closes in on me
until images
    of trees
    and sky
    become
    one
    tiny
    spot
    in the
    pitch-black
    of nothingness.

BEHIND THE TREES

Water splashes on my face.
A voice yells,

"¡Lula, despierta!"

I flutter my eyes.
I see the sky again.
The branches again.
Concha again.

The inferno of air
pushes down against my ribs,
makes me want to throw up.

"What's happening to me, Concha?" The words drip out
of me like water from melting ice.

"You most likely are getting heat stroke, but here, drink
more," she says, pushing Paquita's canteen into my
mouth.

I drink.
I see little fuzzy figures
swooshing by.

Starlings.

Why aren't they consumed by this heat?
I drink. I drink.

Slowly the water fills me.

My head steadies.

Things come to focus

I breathe on pace again.

The clear, peppered song of birds
brightens my vision.

> "That's it, Lula, you're coming back. Hey, can you spot
> me? I need to go pee behind those trees," Concha says
> while she gets up and undoes her pants button.

I nod, noticing where we are.
The water of the irrigation canal glistens.
I can't see Rafa and Papá working,
the grape vines are too lush.

Then, I hear the crushing of leaves
and footsteps two or three rows down.
I don't see anyone
but I know someone is there.

> "Concha, watch out!" my voice shoots out and surprises
> me with how clear it is.

Then the footsteps stop.

> "Who's there?" I demand but I hear no one answer.

Concha comes running out
from behind the trees.

> "Somebody was spying on me," she whispers.

I point to where the sound was coming from.
Suddenly, we hear a man's voice.

"What are you two doing out here? Escaping work, I see!"

It's el mayordomo.
Concha clears her throat
before she answers,

"No, señor. My sister is overheating and she needed to
rest in the shade and drink more water."

"Aquí, there is no rest. You. Are. Here. To. Work." His
voice sounds as harsh as sand.

The veins on his forehead bulge.

"Unless you are here to give me another kind of work."

He slowly walks up to her. His eyes, wicked.

"No, we're going." She helps me up. "Vamos, Lula."

I jump to my feet, propelled
by the fear turning somersaults
in my stomach.
As she reaches for me,
el mayordomo grabs Concha's wrist
and pulls her to him.
She struggles to break free.

I let out a piercing scream.

"Leave me alone, desgraciado!" she yells at him.

"Calma, preciosa. I'm not going to hurt you," he says.

"No! No!" I shout, though my voice breaks in the air into
shattered fragments.

Then suddenly, we hear Papá's whistle
cut clear across the field.

We all turn to the sound.

Did he hear my scream?

Concha tears herself loose
from el mayordomo.

She grabs my hand,
pulls me and yells,

"¡Vamos, Lula! ¡Corre!"

MAMA IN MIND

My side aches.
     Water swishes
          around my full stomach.
     I am nauseous as
we approach Papá.

Concha makes me swear
not to tell Papá about el mayordomo.

     "Why not? He was spying on you and could have—"
     I begin to answer.

     "Lula," she cuts me off, "we don't know what he was
     going to do."

She pauses. Turns down her lips.

     "We have to keep Mamá in mind. We need this work.
     We can't make more trouble than there already is."

     "But he . . ." I push.

     "Lula, promise. Please."

I reluctantly agree.

We don't know how
Papá would respond.

Still, why would we want to protect
a coyote like el mayordomo?

CHEATED

Sixty-eight boxes today
picked, packed, and sorted.

Our family did this together
       despite my heat stroke
       despite the Peeping Tom mayordomo
breathing down our necks.

When el mayordomo pays us,
he counts five boxes less.

Papá shifts his legs,
       folds his arms across his chest
              and asks him to count again.
Out loud this time.

El mayordomo counts
unable to outsmart
Papá's owl-like vision.

    "You packed sixty-eight boxes. But your hijas took a long
    break so I'm paying them for seven hours work, not
    ten," he finally says.

    "They were only gone for an hour at most." Rafa steps
    up to him but then Papá calmly holds Rafa with the
    back of his hand.

    "Escúchame, you will pay us for the time we worked,"
    Papá delivers with his earthen voice.

Papá is acting like el mayordomo
is one of his kids about to get the belt.

> "No, you hear me, peón! I will pay you what I feel like
> paying you!" El mayordomo tries to stand taller and
> puffs out his chest at Papá.

Papá's long legs make him
            tower over el mayordomo.
        Papá looks down
into the small man's squinting eyes,

> "You will pay us or I—"

> "You'll what? Join the Flips on strike?" El mayordomo
> lets out a big laugh.

But then, Papá grabs him by the shirt
and twists it into his clenched fist.
El mayordomo stops laughing
and pops open his eyes
toward his shotgun resting
on some boxes nearby.

Everyone gathers near them.

> "Oye, count my boxes again too!" Josesito demands.

> "And mine while you're at it!" Felipe says.

> "You're Mexican. You shouldn't be cheating your own
> people!" Paquita says.

Concha and Rafa
seem to be holding
their breath like I am.

When el mayordomo sees
that he is outnumbered, he says,

"Está bien, relax. I have it right here."

I almost wish Papà
had whopped him one right across his head,
for what he did to Concha,
and what he wanted to do
to our wages too.

I'm proud of Papá
for standing up
to a cheat like him
but I'm scared that el mayordomo
will never let Concha and me
forget we got away.

TRUCK BED

On the pickup truck
to take us home,
      the calls of starlings   circle above.
They soothe my exhaustion.

No number of scarecrows
      will keep the birds
      from diving
      into the sweet grapes
once we've left.

We drive on the dirt road.
      I lean over the wood railing
        and extend my arms, like a sapling.
I steal this moment for myself.
      I am free here
        feathery wisps of wind
          push lightly
    against my face.

I pretend to be the ringmaster
      making   people bounce with happiness
describing a girl on a trapeze that is also me
      flying   through a circus tent,
    an audience of people roaring
    with applause below.
I am *everyone* in the carpa.

As the vineyards   get smaller
    the bigger   my relief grows
      that the day is over
        and I can   fly away.

BARRACK MEETING I

Later that evening,
Concha and me leave Mamá alone.
Her face is more plump plum than shriveled prune,
which eases our minds enough to take
the babies and follow Rafa and Papá to the meeting
at Josesito's family barrack down the row.

We don't ask Papá if we can go to the meeting.
We don't give him a chance to say no.

When he sees us at the meeting,
Papá narrows his eyes.
I press baby Martín against
my chest to hide my face behind him.

The room is packed with Mexican families.
I don't see Leonor though.

Then, the same dark-haired thin woman
going door to door with Leonor yesterday,
calls everyone's attention
and speaks to us in Spanish.

> "Thank you for coming. My name is Dolores Huerta and
> this is Gil Padilla. We are organizers with the National
> Farm Worker's Association." She speaks firmly. "Brothers
> and sisters, we are out here fighting for the rights of all
> farmworkers. Your rights. We know how hard you work
> for such low wages and how sometimes the growers
> cheat you out of your earnings. We know how terrible
> the conditions are on the fields, under the heat and
> cold, and how difficult it is to live in workers' camps

like this. These are the things we are trying to change,
for the better. We called this meeting because we know
some of you just arrived here and we want to bring you
up to date with the lucha that's taking place."

The room falls silent.
I am mesmerized by the way she speaks.
Like a ringmaster
with fire burning behind her voice.

Gil Padilla follows her,

> "The Filipino workers union went on strike six days ago.
> They're striking for a pay increase from $1.25 to $1.40
> per hour and a piece rate for each box of grapes from
> ten cents to twenty-five cents. They want to pressure
> the growers by not working. You might not know, but
> those of you who have crossed the picket lines are not
> helping the strikers, nor their fight for better pay."

Then Dolores takes the reigns,

> "The National Farm Worker's Association is preparing
> to join them because we deserve the same fair wages
> but . . ." She pauses and looks around the room at every
> person. " . . . we need you to also join la causa. Strength
> in numbers is the only way this is going to work."

The room erupts with discussion.
People ask questions
over one another in a frenzied chatter.

Papá pulls in his lips
and looks away.
I can tell he doesn't agree
by the way his muscles move
along his straining jaw.

BARRACK MEETING II

Then, Paquita holding her son's hand
stands up and asks loudly,

"Who's going to feed my family if we strike?"

"They're just going to hire more workers if we walk off
the job," says Josesito, his mustache twitching.

"They might throw us out of our barracks if we strike.
Where will we go?" says Paquita's sister, Lupe.

Dolores raises both of her hands
as if to say "calm down."

"We have been collecting donations and we're arranging
food caravans so nobody will go hungry. And to answer
your question"—Dolores points at Josesito—"they might
get more workers but we'll just have to talk to them
like we are doing here today. I can tell you that we
won't go without a fight."

Papá rises, bigger
than most of the men here,
and asks,

"What if the growers don't give in?"

Dolores pushes on.

"They have to, September is prime picking season. They
don't want their grapes to go bad on the vine. The
more of us strike, the more crops they stand to lose. No

grapes means nothing to sell to the supermarkets and they don't get paid." Dolores addresses not only Papá but everyone. "Listen, the way growers have been treating farmworkers is unfair. We've been organizing people up and down California, hoping to form an official union, and planned to strike in a few years. But since the Filipino workers beat us to strike, this is an opportunity to fight for our wages now and help everyone."

"I don't think we're going to be able to pull it off," says Lupe.

"Yes, we can. Sí se puede. If we do it, together," Dolores says while landing one closed fist into the palm of the other hand.

"I'm in!" say Josesito, standing.

Then Paquita says it too,
      then another and another.
      The whole room slowly
      stands in agreement.

      I am convinced by Dolores!
      By the looks on Concha's and Rafa's faces,
      they are in too.

I can hardly believe
Dolores stood up to Papá.
It's the first time I've seen
any woman do that.

Her words quieted
all the workers who doubted,
all those except Papá
with his sour face.

FORCED TO LEAVE

Papá taps Rafa on the leg.
Rafa sends Concha and me
dart-like looks.
The meeting is over
for our family,
we need to follow
them out.

As we move to leave, Dolores says,

> "We've set up a credit union for those who need to bor-
> row money and we now have a no-cost mobile medical
> clinic with a resident doctor for anyone who needs it."

Papá stops cold.

We all do.

I have a feeling we are
thinking the same thing—Mamá!

> If we join the NFWA
> and the strike,
> then maybe Mamá
> can see a doctor.

WHAT WE NEED

Rafa takes Martín from my arms
when the meeting is over.
I swivel my feet into the dirt
slowly behind them.

My thoughts follow the swirls.

> Dolores stood up to Papá.
> The first time I've seen a woman do that.
> Mamá is so soft-spoken around him.
> If she ever disagrees with him, she hardly shows it.

Dolores knows how much we hurt.
She named each of the things
that make it so hard to be farmworkers
— low wages, the heat, no breaks,
long hours, the pesticides, our run-down barracks.

> The things Concha wants
> to take us away from if she goes to college.
> The things that probably made Mamá sick,
> and make Papá so grumpy and tired all the time.

Dolores wants us to have what we need.
She isn't afraid to fight.

> Her voice remains in my head.
> It blares like a megaphone,
> rises above all the other voices.
> If Dolores wanted, she would make
> a great ringmaster. I'm sure of it.

DAYDREAM

I imagine my voice as strong as Dolores's.

> In the carpa.
> Lights ablaze.
> The audience buzzing.
> Ready in my red jacket with coattails.
> The applause opens my voice.
> I grow loud.
> My every sound echoes.

> > The singer is out sick.
> > So I take her place.
> > I remove my jacket to reveal
> > a gold sequined evening gown.
> > I cue the piano player,
> > clear my throat,
> > and siiing...

Smooth round sounds flow out of me.
> I SING,
> Soaring high and low,
> climbing with melody
> and sliding smoothly
> into the beat..
More than a ringmaster,
I am *the* singer.
The main act.

I am magic and fire,
like Dolores.

NOT WOMEN

Papá paces in our barrack,
he looks full of thoughts
after the meeting.

Papá says Dolores Huerta is a "libertina"
because she tries to do the work of men.

> "What I saw was someone fighting for everyone, Papá,"
> Rafa says.

Papá frowns his disapproval at Rafa.

> "What does it matter anyway, you heard what she said
> about the clinic. It's a chance to get help for Mamá,"
> Rafa says.

> "I'll have to see it to believe it."

Papá almost always agrees with Rafa.
Though he isn't the oldest child,
    Rafa is the oldest boy.
    Rafa's boy words count more
than girl words in our family.

Rafa knows this and he tries
not to make us feel bad
but it still happens
and it snaps twigs of sadness
inside of me each time
Papá is so unfair.

"Dolores said we can go to the association offices in town and get more information," Rafa says.

"Está bien, we'll go, but after work." Papá says.

"Shouldn't we be joining the picket line tomorrow?" Rafa asks.

"Not yet, Rafa. I'm not a man who makes decisions así nomás. Especially coming from some vieja. I've got to talk more to Gil Padilla or to other men to get to the bottom of it."

Rafa doesn't respond anymore.

Concha and I exchange glances.
We know better than to say a word.

ROADSIDE STRIKERS

We enter the harvest
early the next morning
before the sweltering begins.

I worry because we should be striking
like the others in the meeting
but we remain scabs.

We are far from safe
from the spying cheat
of el mayordomo.

I am crouching and cutting
green grapes alongside Concha
when we see cars barreling down
the dirt road toward us.

Filipino men
get out of their cars.
They line the road, holding
picket signs that say "STRIKE AWOC."

They yell,

"Come on out of the fields! Join us! Don't let the growers
take advantage of you!"

Concha whispers, "Strikers."
Her dark eyebrows lift
in a bow of surprise.

Papá is suddenly near us.

El mayordomo approaches
and yells at them
to stop trespassing.

Papá's face curls into a question.
Besides not reading or writing English,
Papá can't speak it either
so he needs us to explain.

"They're asking us to join their strike. They're asking
for fair wages like Dolores said last night," Concha says.

Papá grunts.

"Not yet. Not until I can talk to Gil Padilla or to
Cesar Chávez himself."

"Who's that?" I ask.

"My friends tell me he's the one who's in charge," Papá says.

"What do you think he'll say that's different than
Dolores?" Rafa asks.

"We will soon see."

Rafa's belief in Dolores isn't enough.
I don't understand
what Papá has
against her.

"For now, vamos, a jalar," Papá says.

I look over at Concha.
She taps me on the arm
to hurry me to get to moving.

I go back under the grape leaves
and get to work again
at my sister's side.

I close my eyes once,
take in a big breath of hot dry air,
listen to the shouts of the strikers
and the chirping of starlings.

HEAT SHOT

Soon after, Concha and me
        have left Papá and Rafa
   a few rows behind us
and are now close
to the strikers again.

El mayordomo is gone
        and the strikers' shouts kick back up
but this time, they are even more directed at us.

I keep my head in my work
        and try not to make eye contact.
Could one of them be Leonor's dad
or her titos?

I stack three full wood crates
        of grapes onto others.

      "Come on out. We need your help. Our strikers won
      fair wages in Coachella only a few months ago when
      we all went on strike. We can do it again but we can't
      do this without you."

Suddenly, a green pickup truck
        kicks up a cloud of dust behind it.
It comes closer until it stops.

Six growers get out of the truck,
        holding shotguns.
I know they're growers
        by their white skin and blond hair,
by the like-new collared shirts,
        jeans, and good boots they wear.

Through suffocating heat they shout,

"Pack it up, Flips! Get on out of here!"

The strikers shout back in a chorus,

"Fair wages for fair labor!"

El mayordomo stands beside the growers, his bosses.
Seeing as he couldn't get rid of the strikers,
he must have gone to get them.

The growers and el mayordomo lift their shotguns,
point them at the strikers,
and shivers of fear
move up the ladder of my spine.

Concha suddenly grabs my forearm
and pulls me down and into the thicket
of grape vines to hide.

The growers' shouts intensify.

"You're trespassing."
"Go on, now, get!"

And the strikers' shouts get louder
as they get closer to the growers.

"Give us fair wages!"
"Strike!" "Strike!" "Strike!"

Then, suddenly, the oldest-looking grower shouts,

"I said, get off my property!"

He shoots his shotgun
          twice into the air.

Screams surround me.

I can't move.

The Filipino strikers run to their cars
and pull out shotguns of their own.
          They stand together holding their guns
          across their chests with their heads held high.
          Their eyes locked cold on the growers.

They don't look afraid.

          Then suddenly,
          some of the field workers
run into the surcos.

On that movement,
          growers and strikers start shooting
their shotguns into the air.
The gunshots are so loud,
          I cover my ears
                    and collapse
                    curling
                    into
                    a ball.

I feel Concha drape herself
          over my body
and hug me tightly.

"It's okay. It's okay," I hear her say.

"Concha!" I cry, and squeeze my eyes shut.

"Te tengo, Lula."

And then,

      it is so silent,

the birds no longer sing.

BROTE

You can't reach good ends through evil means,
because the means represent the seed
and the end represents the tree.
—Martin Luther King Jr.

SUSTO

Mamá always gives us
something sweet to eat,
like bread or fruit, after a fright.

She says, "Dulce helps calm a susto."

Concha and I sit in silence and eat grapes.

There is a dull ringing
in my ears from the blasts.

What if someone had been killed?

Inside, I tremble not only from the susto
but from how unfair it all seems to me now.
How unfair it has *always* been for us.

The need to make things right
appears like a new bud in me.

We do have rights, like Dolores said.
We should be paid well for this hard work.
We should be able to take breaks to drink water.
We shouldn't be shot at when we protest.

Papá is the only one
keeping us from striking.

What will we have to do
to change his mind?

A DOCTOR'S TOUCH

As we enter our barrack after work
Mamá frowns slightly in her sleep.
while the babies play on the bed.

A deep wrinkle grows
between her eyebrows.
She's cold and clammy to the touch,
despite the heat.

I resist the urge to jump
into bed with Mamá.
To ask her to hold me
after the day we've had.
She's too weak.

Instead, I dip a tin cup
into our pail of drinking water
and come back with it
dripping from the bottom.

I hear Papá and Rafa outside, talking
with some of the other workers.
about the shoot-out.

Papá's face softens
when he comes in and sees Mamá.

Rafa takes the cup of water from me.
He kneels by Mamá
and holds it near her mouth.

"Mamá. It's Rafa. Please drink. It'll do you good," he
insists, and kisses her softly on the cheek.

Mamá smiles at his kiss
and parts open her eyes.
She sees us all standing above her,
and her smile
widens.

Rafa holds her head up.
His dusty hand
cradles her neck delicately.
He is deliberate and patient
as he returns the cup to her mouth.

He'd be the best person
to nurse Mamá back to health,
but Papá would never allow him
to stay home.

When Mamá is done,
she taps his face sweetly and says,

"Thank you, mi doctorcito."

As good as Rafa is with her,
as much as Doña Serafina's herbs have helped,
Mamá might also need a doctor.

"Papá, we have to take her to the farmworker's clinic,"
I say, not trying to hide how desperate I feel.

His angry eyebrows turn jagged.
He looks at me as if
I've spoken out of line.

"I think we need to be members of the association
first, though," says Rafa.

Papá doesn't respond to us.
He simply grunts,

"Vamos, Rafa."

Rafa looks torn.
But he gives me back the cup,
turns his eyes down to Mamá, strokes her forehead,
and follows Papá out the door.

If they are going to town,
Concha and I are not invited.

I sit on the edge of Mamá's bed,
fold over, and lay my head on her belly,
feel her caress my head.

The susto of the day
a rough rock of fear
trapped in my throat.

I turn away from her
so she doesn't see
the stream of my tears
falling on her blanket.

WHAT HAPPENED?

It is nearly eight o'clock
     when Papá and Rafa return.

The late summer sun is beginning to set.
     The trees and buildings have turned
          to dark brown shadows against
               the orange-pink sky.

The heat is residing,
     a welcome coolness sweeps
          through the air,
               and the buzz of mosquitos
                    is beginning to grow.

A radio plays from the barrack next door.
     The sounds of ranchera music
          toss melodies
               into the cooling air,
                    a happiness that seems
                        so out of reach right now.

Luckily, Concha and me
     have dinner ready for Papá and Rafa.
          We have beans, tortillas, and chile
               to add to the rice Paquita brought over.

Rafa goes to see Mamá, but Papá
     stops outside our barrack
          and sits in a chair near the stove.
He reaches over to light his cigarette
     while Concha and I serve him dinner.

We wait for him to say
        one single word to us
                about what happened
                        at the association offices.

Papá eats in silence but his face looks
        like there is something loud clanking
                inside his mind.

If only
        I could pry open
                his thoughts.

WOMEN'S WORK

With Rafa and other men
Papá is easy as pudding.

Rafa is not expected
to do any cooking,
baby watching, or clothes washing,
though Rafa does it
without being asked
because he knows it's only fair.

Papá always pulls Rafa
from a house chore
to do "boy's deberes"
like go hunt wild rabbits with slingshots
or to fix something that's broken
though we'd like to do that too.

When Concha complains,
Mamá says the home is "woman's work."

      "Así son las cosas."

But I agree with Concha
that's not "just the way things are."

They shouldn't be,
anyway.

MEXICAN INDEPENDENCE

We go inside to hand Rafa
        a plate of food
we served for him too.

He asks us,

      "Did he tell you?"

Concha and I shake our heads
        and look at Papá quietly eating outside.

I can tell Rafa is really hungry too
        by the way he shovels food in his mouth.
He chews, swallows, and then says,

      "On our way to the offices they told us a big meeting
      was happening at the Our Lady of Guadalupe Church
      hall, so we went there instead. The place was packed
      with farmworkers and there was even a band playing
      because it's Mexican Independence Day."

      "Oh yeah, dieciséis de septiembre," Concha says.

      "Some people were making speeches and answering
      everyone's questions. Dolores Huerta was there, so was
      that man, Cesar Chávez."

      "What'd she say?" Concha asks.

      "They said huelga is one of the most powerful weapons
      workers have. It doesn't matter if another union started

it, if the Mexicans don't join the Filipinos, then they
will get the benefits of it and we will be left out."
"So are we joining?" Concha asks with urgency.

Rafa nods, his words muffled
    by his chewing.

        "Mm-hmm. Papá let us join."

        "Us too?" I chime in.

        "Yeah, I guess so. And supposedly, the NFWA is organiz-
        ing to help workers either find other work on other
        farms, or inside the organization."

Concha's question bumps into mine:

        "When does the strike start?"
        "Where's our first strike?"

Rafa puts up his hand,
    his palm facing us,
telling us to wait as he swallows.

        "It's starting tomorrow and I'm not sure. We'll
        know when they come for us."

        "How do you get a job with the NFWA?" Concha asks.

        "I'm not sure but it pays five dollars a week, which is
        what everyone who works for the union gets paid, even
        Cesar and Dolores themselves."

"That's not very much," Concha says.

"I know, we'd have to tighten up."
"Tighter than we already are?" she argues.

"Remember, Dolores said we have to make sacrifices for
la causa."

"Right, the cause, our purpose for the greater good,"
Concha says.

"What about the clinic? What about Mamá?" I ask.

"Dolores Huerta gave me the location of where the clinic
is going to be stationed. Tomorrow, I'm going to see if I
can find a ride to take Mamá there. Papá's going to the
picket line."

Papá walks in then and Concha asks,

"Can Lula and I come to the picket line with you?"

Papá stops and looks up at Concha
like she just offended him and says, "No."

That cold and brief no is enough
                    to hush our questions
                                back into silence.

AGAINST PAPÁ

I'm still shaken
about what happened today.
If we aren't working or picketing,
I want to go to school.

I don't say this out loud.
It seems too selfish a thought
to think right now.

Papá says,

>"You girls will stay to take care of things at home,
>como debe ser."

As it should be?

My face flushes with frustration
when he shuts us down like this.

Now I don't want to go to school at all
but to the picket line to raise our voices
like Dolores said we should.

Doesn't he think we have rights too?

If Mamá weren't sick,
I'd probably be going on strike
against Papá.

MIND GLIMPSE

I never remember my dreams.

Mornings, I catch glimpses in my mind.

A hot-air balloon sailing over an ocean.

Or Papá in black and white,
his hair coated in hair oil.

Sunflowers singing in the sun.

A field of dancing quelites waving,
their leaves like arms with the wind.

Chubby babies walking in a line behind Mamá.

Seeds growing roots inside the earth.

None are ever about the circus.

This could be why
I hold my daydreams so close.

Nothing fades.

They come alive with wild color,
with glitter,   with laughter,   with lights.

I take my place on the stage.
I stand upright like a light post.
The entire show relies on me.

I know each of their acts,
      the timing of clowns,
      the routine of dogs,
      the speed and tricks of horses,
      the twirl of dancers,
      the sway of trapeze artists,
      the music of singers.

My voice swims through the crowd
      with elegance and suspense.
         It rivets and captures,
            takes hold of viewers
            and wraps them
            into the wonder
            before them.

         My one and only perfect voice
         is the reason
         the show goes on.

TAPPING IN

Leonor is at the tap
the next morning, in line
for water, when I walk up.

She seems bothered.
When I ask her what's wrong,
she doesn't hear me the first time,
so I ask again.

Her parents didn't let her go
to the picket line with them today,
the same as me.

Leonor's engine is revving up,

> "They said we should act like nothing's happening.
> But there's a big strike going on and I want to be
> there too! Especially after what the growers did
> yesterday. Maybe they won't shoot if there are kids
> around?"

> "I'm not so sure about that, I was there and they shot
> their guns. It was the scariest thing, Leonor!" I say.

> "You were? That's wild! But my dad said now that Mexicans
> have joined, there will be safety in numbers. They can't
> shoot one hundred or one thousand of us, right?"

An idea pops into my head . . .

What if Leonor and I walk over
to the strike together?

Though the growers are angry
and Papá said we couldn't go,
we *have* to do something.

Maybe he won't see me
if there are one thousand people
there like Leonor said.

I whisper my idea into Leonor's ear.

    "I like the way you think," she says, and taps my back.

Leonor says they'll be
at the Tulare farm,
only a couple of farms over
and not too far of a walk.

When I make my case with Concha
she doesn't like it at all—she's too scared for me.
After lots of begging, she finally agrees
        I can hide
        as small as I am
        inside the bigness
        of a crowd.

I'm almost more afraid
of Papá than the growers.

GIRLS CAN

Tulare farm is farther than I expect
but it's okay because Leonor talks non-stop.

Each time I try to say something
her mouth engine takes off.

She tells me about her uncles
who live in the men's barracks.

They came here from the Philippines
without their families, just like her dad.

They call themselves "Manong"
and not Filipino like everyone else does.

Not "Flip" because it's a bad word
to call them, like "Spik" is to us.

Her dad met her Mexican mom
while working on the fields.

Then Leonor drifts into talking about her dream
to be a commercial pilot when she grows up.

> "I'm not even scared. I want to be up so far in the sky!
> Just imagine what that would feel like?"

I've never seen or read about a girl pilot:
I guess there is no harm done in dreaming.

Just like I've never known of a girl ringmaster
but I dream about it anyway.

THE SPRAYERS

The only planes
Leonor and me
have ever seen up close
are those that fly
over the fields spraying
the crops for bugs.

When I tell Leonor
we think some of what
they sprayed got on Mamá
made her sick,
Leonor says,

>"I could have told you that! Those sprayers are no good
> and not only because of what they spray either."

Leonor tells me about her cousin Jesús
who wanted to be a pilot too
after he got a job standing
on the edge of the field waving a red cloth
to help the pilot know
where to stop spraying.

One day, the plane got too low
as it turned around
and clipped him in the head
and killed him right there.

I stop walking,
hold Leonor's arm,
and look at her.
 "I'm sorry"

are the only words
I can find to say.

> "Yeah. He was only sixteen. But that's why I wanna fly. I
> want to do what he didn't get to do. Who knows, maybe
> he'll see me flying a plane from up in heaven," she says,
> smiling.

We hear faint shouting.
We look at each other.
Leonor's mouth drops open.

My heart is a galloping horse
inside my chest
because we're getting close.

But then that happy gallop
inside my heart turns to stone.
I get so nervous Papá might see me,
my legs stop moving.

Leonor looks back
and waves me toward her,
she points to a sign that reads: "Tulare County."

> "Let's go, Lula! We're almost there!"

I inhale a big gulp of warm air
and I begin
to walk again.

CAMOUFLAGE

I count maybe thirty strikers,
      not the thousand
      we imagined.

Their bodies take up little room,
      are bunched up,
      and move against
      the vastness of the fields.

I squint my eyes to see
      if I can make out
      Papá's figure.

Nothing.

Still, we approach cautiously,
      hiding behind a line of cars
      parked along the road.

The strikers are staying off the farm's property.
      Maybe they don't want the growers
      getting mad about them trespassing again.

The strikers are Manong men like yesterday.
      But there are also Mexicans and some women
      with their *children*, too!

These men must not have rules like Papá.
A white man with a fancy camera takes pictures.
      When I see him,
      I duck lower behind a car.

The last thing I need
     is evidence
     I was here.

Leonor spots her parents
     and some of her uncles.

She nudges me gently with her elbow,

     "Look, there's my tito Larry. Larry Itliong. He started
     this whole thing."

I recognize him from the shoot-out!
     I can tell he's serious about the strike
     because he's talking directly
     with one group of picketers before
     going on to the next.

There's a crowd of men on the far end.
     I think I see Papá's hat
     in their huddle
     but I can't be sure because
     they're all wearing sombreros.

I tremble with regret.
     I shouldn't have come.
     I want to be like a praying mantis
     and camouflage myself into the cars
     for protection.
I freeze when Leonor suggests,

     "Let's get closer, Lula!"

WHAT THE PICKET SIGNS READ:

"DELANO GRAPE STRIKE AWOC AFL-CIO"

"NFWA AND AWOC AFL-CIO STRIKE TOGETHER"

"FARMWORKERS DESERVE COLLECTIVE BARGAINING"

"PICKET"

"DON'T BE A SCAB"

"¡ÚNANSE A NOSTROS!"

"NON-VIOLENT STRIKERS"

and "¡HUELGA!"

BULLHORN

Out of the corner of my eye, I see Dolores.
>   She's yelling into a cone made of newspaper
>   that looks to be a copy of *El Malcriado*.

There is that powerful voice again.
>   Quick and strong, rushing
>   into the makeshift bullhorn,
>   pouring out a waterfall of words:

>   "Come on out, brothers! We are waiting for you. You are
>   earning more money today because our brothers went
>   out on strike on September eighth and they are still out
>   on strike. Does it make you feel better that you are tak-
>   ing their job? Don't be a traitor against us. Come on out
>   and help the strikers because only in solidarity there is
>   strength!"

Leonor points at Dolores and says,

>   "She organized with my tito Larry in the CSO. The
>   Manongs like her. She knows what she's doing."

I don't understand what Leonor means
by CSO but it doesn't matter
>   because right now,
>   I only see Dolores.

The workers move away from the road.
Dolores stops suddenly.
>   She grabs a sign and her newspaper bullhorn and
>   climbs onto an old panel truck,
>   her face pursed with determination.

Someone yells,

> "She's climbing la perrera!" I'm guessing that's the
> nickname of the old truck.

She's as quick to climb
> as she is speaking
> and continues right where she left off.

> "Farmworkers need bathrooms in the fields. You need
> breaks and to be given water. The sun will dry you up
> like raisins if you don't drink. You need to feed your
> children. Do you want them to live in the misery they
> live in now? Don't you want a better future for them?"

Some of the workers turn their heads to Dolores,
much more visible now
> because she is up high on the truck,
> and they pause.

The picketers watch her too.

The cameraman
> turns his camera
> to her slender figure
> towering above us.

She is like a ringmaster up on a stage
> pulling us into the spell of her performance.

Her voice booms.

> "Farmworkers deserve to share in the richness we help
> produce. Join us, brothers and sisters, join us!"

She puts her makeshift bullhorn down
  and lifts her cardboard sign
  above her head.
  The sign is painted black with big
  white capital letters and reads:

  "HUELGA."

She stares silently at the workers
  with a furrowed brow and beaming eyes
  that say as much as her words.

She hushes us in that stance.

We are all captivated by Dolores,
  who seems larger and mightier
  than the mountains beyond us.

All I hear is
  the click and wind,
  click and wind
  of the camera.

Cheers break out suddenly.
  The workers drop their tools,
  they move out of the fields
    and come toward the pickets!

The scabs' stern faces
    bloom into smiles,
    welcomed by picketers
    who are holding cards
    and yelling,

"Sign your pledge to strike here!"

"Over here, get your union card!"

Others are screaming and a chorus responds,

"¡Que viva el campesino!"

"¡Que viva!"

"¡Que viva la huelga!"

"¡Que viva!"

"¡Que viva la causa!"

"¡Que viva!"

I count the workers again.
Thirty-six . . . Forty-one . . .
Fifty-three . . . Eighty-eight!

In this cloud of joy,
I am overcome by a thought —maybe I don't want to be
a ringmaster after all
but an organizer
as fierce as Dolores.

CAUGHT ON THE LINE

Leonor bursts out
> from behind the car
> and runs to her parents,
>> who are clapping
>> and congratulating the new strikers.

Her mother frowns at her at first
> but seems too happy with all the people
> who have come off the fields.
> She shakes her head at Leonor
> but rubs her back lovingly.

> "Lula!" I hear my name.

My heart drops into my stomach.
It's Papá's unmistakably deep voice.

> "Qué fregados are you doing here?"

I close my eyes and don't answer.

> "Lula! I'm talking to you!"

I take a big breath and then turn slowly.

Papá stands with his arms crossed,
> leaning more on one of his legs.
>> His head is tilted back and he glares
>> all the way down at me.
>> All
>> the way
>> down.

I shrink
from a floating cloud
into a droplet of water
that will soon
evaporate.

PAPÁ'S PERFORMANCE

"Who told you it was okay to come?" Papá's
shout rumbles inside me.

I lower my head, look at
my old dirt-covered shoes.

"I'm sorry, Papá. Nobody. Nobody let me come . . ."

My voice fades behind
Papá's frustration.
Plus, I don't want Concha
to get in trouble because of me.

The workers coming off the field
did not sweep him up into their happiness.

We are the only people not smiling.

"You seem to have forgotten your place, Lula."

"Pero Papá, there are women out here. Look at what
Dolores just did . . ."

I begin to argue
but he silences me
by clucking his tongue
inside his mouth.

"No excuses. You disobeyed me. I said I did not want you
and Concha on the picket line. Don't you remember what
happened yesterday? These growers think we are basura
and they will get rid of us no matter if you are a man,
woman, or child."

I search the crowd for Dolores.
  I wish that she would see Papà's rising anger.
  But I don't see her
  now that she's off the truck.

  "Sí, Papá," I answer.

  "Te me vas. You will go, ¡ahora mismo!"

He points back toward home.

Just then, Leonor pulls her mother
  by the hand to Papá and me.

  "I'm Leonor, Lula's friend from school. This is my Mamá,
  Socorro De la Cruz, and my dad is somewhere over
  there." She smiles up at Papá.

Then the manners Papá reserves for others
  appear out of nowhere.
  He smiles without showing any teeth
  and shakes Leonor's mom's hand.

He tells her it's nice to meet her
  in a honey-sweet way
  as if he wasn't scolding me
  just a few seconds ago.

  "Mamá, this is my new friend Lula," says Leonor.

  "Mucho gusto, Lula. Leonor's told me all about you."

Socorro De la Cruz speaks English and Spanish,
  but is as mexicana as Mamá, who only speaks Spanish.

Leonor and her mom share the same high cheekbones
and eyebrows—full dark arches that decorate
their small foreheads.

"Mucho gusto, señora," I say with my tiny voice.

"I'm glad you've found each other. Diosito knows that it's
hard finding friends when everyone moves so much."
Señora De la Cruz says to us in Spanish.

"Lula was just heading back home," Papá says with a
soft but firm tone.

"Why don't you girls walk back together? Go on now,
you weren't supposed to be here, Leo," Señora De la
Cruz says.

"That's a great idea," Papá says between his teeth as he
fakes a smile.

He won't even look at me now.

Leonor's mamá takes my hand
        in one of hers
        and taps it gently with the other.
Her face is in disbelief.

"Girls," Señora De la Cruz says with the look of happiness and disbelief, "we just witnessed a major victory.
The road might be long, but we can only pray it'll get
better from here on out."
I feel flutters inside me.
        They make my heart rise

from my stomach
and find its rightful place
inside my chest.

Leonor grabs me by the arm and says,

"Come on, Lula! I'll race you back!"

SCARED STRIDES

I run after Leonor.
  I don't say goodbye to Papá.
  I don't want to see
  his disapproving face.
  I don't want to think
  about what kind of golpes
  he'll give me
  when we get home.

I push my body into the heavy heat
  of the early afternoon
  crashing against my fear.

I don't care if Leonor sees me.

  I am opened wide.

  My tears roll
  onto my cheeks.
  Rows after rows
  of grapevines pass me
  as my feet lift off
  the ground
  and press against
  the earth
  with each
  of my
  strides.

CAPULLO

One tiny bean seed holds the possibility
of endless abundance.
—Rowen White

HOLDING BARRACK

Our barrack is as empty
        as my stomach.
Mamá and Rafa must have
gone to the clinic, but where
are Concha and the babies?

My panza growls like a rabid dog.
I don't know which is bigger inside me,
        my hunger or my fear of what
        Papá will do to me when he gets home.

Mamá says the rich people
who enslaved Papá
when he was a boy
beat him if he ever disobeyed.

        They would tie him to a tree,
        whip him with sturdy branches till he bled,
        and leave him there tied up all night.

This was his punishment.

Mamá says the worst we'll ever get
        is a spanking, like her abuela gave to her
        but that she has never given to us.

After what I've done today,
        I'm afraid Papá will not
        hold back.

DRIVEN HOME

A car comes to a stop
in front of our barrack.

Concha and Rafa help Mamá get out
of a station wagon driven by a woman.

I move to grab Gabi and Martín,
whose little expressions are tender with concern.
When Martín sees me, he reaches for me.
Gabi doesn't wait to ask. She simply climbs
my side to find my waiting hip.
Their weight together makes me wobble.

Mamá takes steps carefully,
still too weak to walk without help.
She blinks slowly and nods,
tries to smile for me.

I feel a pinch in my heart
to see her hurting like this
and a pang of guilt because
I wasn't with them.

"Thank you for driving us. We've got it from here,"
Concha says to the driver woman.

When I ask Concha who that is,
she says she's a volunteer for the NFWA clinic.

I hold open the door
and let Mamá in.

CLINICAL MAMÁ

Mamá's body is a slow
        drip of honey
as she lies down and says,

        "I'm so tired."

Rafa makes her comfortable
        by propping her head up
        on two pillows.

                I pull Concha to the side
                to ask what the doctors had to say.

She tells me they didn't see
a doctor but nurses who
couldn't tell them much until
the results of tests they gave her come back.

They say they suspect
Mamá's been exposed to Parathion,
a pesticide they spray in the fields.

        "So, Doña Serafina was right?" I ask.

        "We can't be sure just yet. But they did say we should
        keep giving her Doña Serafina's herbs because they
        seem to be working. She's better off than others they've
        seen."

        "Concha, do people die because of Parathion?"

"They said they've known of one death, a little boy, but
most people recover within two to five months depend-
ing on how bad it is."

"They also noticed a rash on her arms and neck," she
adds, concern growing across her face.

"They said it looks cancerous but the tests will tell us for
sure," Rafa says.

I start to cry
        because I know cancer is something
        that sometimes kills people.
Both Concha and Rafa shake their heads at me.
        I swallow my tears and nod
        when I realize they don't want
        to worry Mamá.

Then I ask them another question.

"Did they ask you for money?"

"That's probably the only good news," Rafa says,
"the clinic is free for all members of the association."

PAPÁ ARRIVES

The sun is diving into the horizon
when Papá comes home.
I expect him to smell like sour liquor
because he's been gone so long,
but he doesn't stumble or sway
or smell in the slightest.

He enters holding his straw hat
in his hand against his chest.
He moves quietly,
his head slightly lowered
as if trying to make himself small
to approach Mamá.

Tremors climb my skin like ants
waiting for him to tear into me.
Concha looks at me strangely.
I haven't told her about the strike
because we've been busy with Mamá.

Papá focuses on Mamá.
Under his arm, he carries two picket signs.
One of them is hidden but the other says:

"NONVIOLENT STRIKERS."

He sits down next to Mamá
and moves a strand of hair away
from her face with the lightest touch.
He whispers,

"Viejita."

Without opening her eyes,
she reaches to find him.
He grabs hold of her fingers
and kisses the top of her hand.
He places it down on the bed again.

"Descansa," he says, and gets up to let her rest again.

He looks at Rafa.
He throws his eyes at the door,
which is his silent way of asking him
to follow him outside.

When they the leave the room,
Concha pinches me and says,

"Why are you shaking, Lula?"

I tell her what happened today
and I can't stop the tears from welling up.
Concha holds my hand tightly and says,

"I won't let him hit you. I'll take the beating before you."

I am grateful for my older sister.
I know she will protect me
but I don't want her to take
a beating that belongs to me.
I disobeyed Papá.
I should be the one to pay.

BEATING BACK VIOLENCE

When I'm about to speak again,
Concha places one finger over my mouth.

"Sh. Papá's telling Rafa where he was."

We listen.

"I spoke to Cesar himself tonight." Papá pauses and then
continues, "He's a real humble man."

"Where did you see him?"

"All of the picketers went down to the Filipino
Community Hall. They've got a mess hall set up for
anyone who pickets. He was there compartiendo,
eating with the rest of us."

"What'd they have to say?"

"Cesar said that he's learned from someone named Gandhi
about the virtue of never lifting a hand in anger, hijo.
That's what he wants for the movement."

Rafa says something that I can't make out
because someone's shuffling their feet.

"And you know what, I almost acted in violence today."

"Was there trouble on the picket again?" Rafa asks.

"The only trouble came from your sister Lula. She
disobeyed me and went to the picket line with her

amiguita. I almost took out the belt and gave her a
good golpiza right then and there. The only thing that
stopped me was the vergüenza I felt for having such a
disobedient daughter."

Rafa doesn't respond.

"I had a mind to come home and teach her a lesson, I
was so angry, but after talking to Cesar, I'm glad I didn't
hit her and won't do it now. I'm trying to
understand what I sow each time I've laid hands on you."

Concha's mouth drops open like mine.
I cover my mouth to stop from crying.
I can't imagine what Rafa must be thinking.

If I ever get to meet this Cesar Chávez man,
I'm going to have to thank him
for whatever he said to Papá.
He saved me from what I thought
was going to be the worst
beating of my life.

SEED BLESSINGS

As September slips into
October like folded hands,
Papá's fury has begun to fade
and the strike continues.

Papá and Rafa are on the picket
every day now and we live
on their five dollars a week each.
Papá seems happier not bending
his breaking back in the fields.

Their wages are only enough to pay
the monthly rent for our barrack.
As donations pour in from outside
Delano, we are lucky to get food
at the strike pantry.

Mamá is a little stronger now,
so Papá agreed to let Concha and me
return to school if we promise
to stay off the picket.

Rafa would like to stay home
because Mamá perks up with his care,
but Papá wants Rafa to be a "real man"
and to defend the strike.

Papá is drinking less now.
Maybe it was learning
about Mamá's poisoning
or maybe it was the strike.

I'm afraid to trust
that the beast inside Papá
is really gone for good.

For now, I hold our blessings
like a bundle of new seeds
in the curl of my hands.

QUELITE STRONG

Mamá is healing.
She wakes
with the morning
better each day
and I fill with sunshine.

She stumbles less,
she cooks a bit,
shows us joy again,
and we circle her
with the laughter
she taught us.

Mamá is quelite strong,
a resilient green
from which we feed
from which we live
and thrive in happiness
and love despite it all.

LEONOR'S RADIO

Leonor listens to her parents' radio
while washing clothes
in a big tin basin outside her barrack
just as I come over with
Gabi and Martín for a visit.

She's singing to a smooth
rhythm and blues song,

> "People get ready,
> there's a train a-coming . . ."

But she sounds like me sometimes
a quacking duck stuck in muck
and I giggle to hear her strange sounds.

> "Come on, Lula! Sing with me!" she says, laughing with me
> and pushing her hands into the wet clothes.

I shake my head, my chuckle winding down,
though I really want to sing too.
Plus, I don't know many songs
because we don't own a radio.

When I had a good, strong voice,
Mama and I used to sing while
we worked in the fields.
Most of the songs I know
are boleros and rancheras
or the Ave María church songs
she taught me.

But now, with this scratchy,
raspy, wispy voice,
I don't have the nerve to sing
so others can hear me.

I bury my voice
into my lungs
because I don't
want to sound
like a duck.

ON MY MIND

The DJ comes on
bursting with excitement.

> "That inspiration of a song, 'People Get Ready,'
> was from none other than the musical group the
> Impressions, featuring Curtis Mayfield. And up next is
> a new little ditty sung by the magnificent voice of Joan
> Baez, with 'Daddy You've Been on My Mind.'"

From the small radio
sitting on an empty chair near Leonor,
a guitar starts strumming, then,
comes a voice so pure and so beautiful,
it makes me want to cry.

The words of the song
make me think of Papá
though they aren't written for him.

Her voice sends me
swimming into a daydream
of one day singing like her.

> "She's Mexican, you know!" Leonor shouts over the music.

I am snapped out of the spell
of Joan Baez's music
and nod and smile at Leonor,
not allowing for that daydream
to float too far away.

TO TOWN

It's Saturday. I wish I could be with Papá and Rafa at the picket line especially because there is no school today.

I tell Rafa to look out for Dolores and to tell me everything he sees when he gets home.

Concha rushes me to finish our chores so we can look for a ride to the food pantry.

When I hesitate to leave Mamá, she says,

> "We'll take the babies to give Mamá a break. Besides,
> I need you to help me because we might have to
> forage for food if there isn't enough at the pantry.
> And nobody forages quite like you, chamaca," she pulls
> playfully on my ear.

We grab an old potato sack to carry back whatever we are able to find.

We swerve around kids playing kick the can, and mothers washing clothes or cooking in their outdoor stoves.

It seems there are more people here than usual. Half the camp must be striking.

I see Leonor climbing onto the back of a truck with her family.

> "Let's ask Leonor!" I say excitedly to Concha.

PICKUP TRUCK CHEERLEADERS

We scramble up on the bed,
>> babies and all.
>> I peek through
>> the cabin of the truck
>> and see several Manong men
>> sitting up front.

Leonor says,

>> "That's my dad and my titos."

The pitter-patter of Leonor's talking
>> is hard to hear over the blowing wind
>> and the blasting rock and roll playing
>> on the truck radio in the cabin up front.

As we pass the different farms,
>> we slow whenever we see a picket line.
>>> Leonor's dad, Mr. De La Cruz, starts honking
>>> and everyone in the back of the truck
>>> hollers, waves, and cheers
>>> for the picketers.

They answer with the same enthusiasm,
>> lifting their picket signs in the air.
>>> We pass a dozen farms
>>>> and a dozen pickets!
Excitement buzzes inside me
>> like a hive at its peak.

One of the pickets we pass is Papá's.
>> They've only got about ten people

but Gil Padilla, the man who came
to the house meeting with Dolores,
is leading them in a good chant.

"¡Que viva la huelga! ¡Que viva!"

Concha yells at Papá as we drive away.

"¡Vamos al mercado!"

Papá smiles at us and waves too.
     He must feel good
          we are doing the things
          he expects from us.

I'd rather be
     fighting on the picket
     screaming "¡Que viva la causa!"
     into a bullhorn
     with them.

If my voice
would let me.

SWELTERING RAINBOW

We look for Albany Street
when we get dropped off
in sweltering downtown Delano.
We find the NFWA offices
because of its sign that reads:

"National Farm Workers Association—Asociación de
Campesinos"

The line for the food pantry
wraps long against the street.
I hold on to Gabi's hand
to stop her from running off.
Martín points and blabbers,
straddled on Concha's hip.

Sweat drips down my temples
as we wait in the unforgiving sun.
I still have a hard time believing
we get this food for free.

When we finally get to the front,
a group of women help us.
Concha pulls out Papá and Rafa's union cards
and hands them to our attendant.

The round-faced woman
takes the cards and says,

"Do these belong to somebody in your family?

"Yes, they're our father's and brother's," Concha replies.

"Do you girls work the fields?" she asks, and furrows her
  eyebrows.

"Yes," we answer in unison, though Concha's voice domi-
  nates mine.

"You should really have your own cards, then."

"We didn't know we could. We thought it was only for
the men on strike," Concha says.

"Of course you can. After we take care of you here, you
girls can go over to the association offices and ask for
Esther or Helen. They'll sign you right up." She smiles
at us. "So, what can we get for you?"

People mill around us.
Their spirits are a splash of colors.
The yellow rays of the pantry line,
the red murmurs in the offices,
the indigo glow of women, helping everyone.
It is all as vibrant as a rainbow
dancing across the clouds.

It makes me forget
my sweating skin.

Delano is sweltering with heat
not only because of the sun.

153

TWO CARD-CARRYING MEMBERS

I suggest to Concha that we not tell Papá we're card-carrying members until we're sure he won't get mad. We decide not even to show them to Rafa in case it slips out before we're ready. Turns out, the NFWA offices are run mostly by women. We meet Esther Urunday first and then Helen Chávez, who is Cesar Chávez's wife, but don't meet him or see Dolores. Concha gets to talking to a secretary her age named Abby, who wears a miniskirt with sandals, liquid eyeliner that makes her eyes look like cat eyes, and a fancy ponytail that poofs at the top of her head. Abby is friendly but hushes us briefly as she turns up her radio.

She listens to news about the Vietnam War because she says her brother is there fighting on the front lines. In the fields, we don't hear too much about the war and I wonder if Rafa will have to go fight when he gets to be eighteen. After the news report is over, she tells Concha about an official high school in Delano where she can go, and that the NFWA is hiring more secretaries who can speak both English and Spanish. They'll teach her how to write shorthand too. I see sparks shooting off in Concha's eyes. We get our cards, agreeing to pay later without knowing how we'll do it.

CONCHA SHARP

Papá lets Concha transfer
to Delano High School
only because of the job
after school at the NFWA offices.

As an after-school secretary,
working for Esther in membership,
she brings in five dollars more,
which makes Papá happy
so long as she's off the picket.
Though she has to leave the barrack
extra early to catch a ride with picketers
and comes back on the bus after dinner.

She studies late into the night.
I sit by her and try to do the same
but her twelfth-grade work
and college applications take longer.

I make us yerba buena tea
from mint I scavenge in the fields
to keep our minds sharp
and to help Mamá too.

It's hard to stay up with Concha.
So, I drift into our bed
when I'm tired
with the rest of the family
and get lulled to sleep by the
soft yellow light of her lantern.

PATIENCE

In school,
we don't learn about
      la huelga,
      nonviolence,
      Martin Luther King, Jr., or Gandhi
      like we read in *El Malcriado*.

In school,
      brown and poor people
      working the fields,
      like us
      don't exist
      in the textbooks.

In school,
we learn about
      Louis & Clark,
      Civil War generals,
      the Gold Rush,
      and United States presidents.

Concha reminds me
what we learn in school,
as wrong as it may seem,
      will bear fruit
      one day.

She's right:
We're farmer workers.
      We know the patience it takes
      to watch plants
      grow.

PICKET DITCH

October Santa Ana winds
sweep at my feet as I walk to school
and I wonder if the same wind
will bring back my voice.

I hear Leonor call my name.
She's in a car full of women.

>"Lula, you want to join us?" she says as she jumps out of
>the car and walks over to me.

>"I . . . I . . . don't know," I stutter.

The thought of going to picket makes my face hot.

>"My mom thought you might want to come along," she
>says, pointing back at the car.

>"But school," I say.

>"Never mind that. La huelga's what matters now!"

I *should* be at the picket
especially now that I've got my card.
I dip my hand into my satchel
>>pull it out,
>>and sheepishly show it to Leonor.

Leonor's face opens like popcorn.

>"Ah! You see, you're meant for the picket. Come on!"

A twisting feeling rushes through me
like a flock of wild canaries
through the trees
as I follow Leonor to the car.

The women are talking loudly
when I hop in and sit by Leonor.

Then suddenly I worry that maybe
they'll ask me to actually use my voice
to speak to the strikers.
Or scream "huelga".

My shoulders bunch up
like stones against my neck.

What if I can't yell
or convince a single soul
to come off the fields?

WHICH STRIKE?

I didn't ask Leonor
to which picket line
we were going.

When we drive up,
    I see Papá from behind.
    I know it's him because
    I recognize the exact place
        where his hat is torn
        like a mouse hole on the brim.

My stomach spirals.
    Why, of all the pickets in Delano,
    did we have to come to Papá's picket?

I can't move.
Leonor and the women spread out
and enter the picket line effortlessly.
    I scoot down in the back seat,
    crouch into my torso, and watch.

Rafa is here too.
    I take a deep breath
    Maybe things won't go
    as badly this time around.

I'm mesmerized by Papá's voice
as it booms in Spanish
into the electric bullhorn.
    He's talking to the scabs working the field.
    He speaks with urgency and clarity
    like I've never seen Papá do.

"My fellow workers, we want you to know our struggle
is not with you, it's with the growers. Don't support a
cheap grower, join our alliance. Those growers don't
need you as much as we need you right now. Maybe
you say, someone else is going to win my battles, and I
am going to gain by it. But that's not the point. If
everyone thought that way, there wouldn't be a strike.
We'd still be in the same lousy condition we were."

The scabs look out at Papá,
      some shrug their shoulders,
      shake their heads, and smile,
           brushing him off.

Papá raises his eyebrows at Rafa.
      Rafa takes the bullhorn from Papá
      and he tries in English.

"Don't believe the propaganda of the growers. Come to
help us with this huelga. They know that in order for
them to make the most money they've got to keep you
down. This is a movement for the people. A nonviolent
movement that wants to hurt nobody. We only want
what is best for our families."

Then, one of the women
who came with us
takes the bullhorn from Rafa.
In Spanish, she says,

"That's right, my comrades, this young man is
telling it like it is. I have broken my back on these
fields alongside you. All, for what? So I can feed my

children. But you know and I know that what they give us is not enough. There is no way out of this poverty if we don't come together. We need you to come out, comrades. What will you tell your children when they get older and can understand? Will you tell them that you fought for a better life or that you looked away from the opportunity for a real future for your family? Help us, the time is now!"

Some of the women begin to chant,

"¡Huelga, huelga, huelga!" and the entire picket joins along.

I don't realize that I'm now
     fully upright
and hanging from the window
         to get a good look.

Papá turns just at that moment.

    He sees me.
        His eyes are two locks
        pressing down on my own.

        I want for my body to run
        but it betrays me.

Before I know it, Papá is at the car
        grabbing my arm to get me out.

    "¡Bájate! Get out of there, now!" he rages. "How dare you disobey me twice, Lula! Who do you think you are? Eh?"

I don't have time to answer
        because I'm out of the car,
                folding into the pain
        of his tight grip on my arm.

That's when I hear Rafa.

        "Apá, calm down. Apá, por favor. Remember what Señor
        Chávez said, 'Never lift a fist in anger,' Apá!"

I look around and realize
        that nobody sees nor hears us.
        The chants of "huelga" drown out
        all other sounds.

Papá turns to Rafa and just as I think
        he is going to hit Rafa too,
        Papá pauses.

Something comes over him.

He lets go of my arm,
throwing it angrily away.

                I don't cry.

        My body is too shocked,
        too scared, or overwhelmed
        by the rattling of my skin,
        the pounding of my blood
        right where Papá let go.

I quickly think to reach
        into my satchel.
        I pull out my membership card.

He doesn't take it but Rafa does.
Rafa's face beams.

> "Papá, take a look. Lula's joined the strikers! She's got a card, she's official!"

Papá is confused and says,

> "With whose money?" His face unravels from the anger.

> "Concha's paying our dues," I manage to say.

> "Papá, she should be able to stay. She's part of us now," Rafa urges. "Her voice counts just like everyone's on this picket line."

He looks at Rafa and then at me and says,

> "Está bien." He doesn't look totally convinced but turns around and walks back to the shouting picket.

Rafa hugs me and taps me on the back.

> "Boy, Lula! That was a close one. But he can't stop you now! Welcome to the NFWA, hermanita!"

My shaking slows.
    I take soft steps after Rafa,
                    exhausted.
I didn't realize speaking up
for yourself took so much effort.

Shouts of "huelga" ring louder
      the closer I get.

            They fill my head,
            roll into my throat,
            and I sing in a whispery canto,

   "¡Huelga! ¡Huelga! ¡Huelga!"

            The lyrics to the song
            of the battle
            I just won.

FLOR

...seeds are going to flower and the spring
is going to come back. But we know we
have to go out there and do all the work.
—Dolores Huerta

FALL FORWARD

We fall into November
        like grape leaves
leaving the vines.

Concha shares with us the changes
        happening at the offices of the NFWA
before we read them in *El Malcriado*.

All the farmworkers in Delano
        —Manong, Arab, Oakie, Mexican, Negro, Puerto Rican—
now make over 2,000 workers on strike!
        There *is* strength in numbers.

Cesar Chávez, Leonor's tito Larry Itliong,
        and Dolores Huerta are up front and leading us.
Though the growers now have the police on their side,
        and the growers bring in busloads of scabs
to break the strike, the leaders never let us think
        our lucha for fairness will go in vain.

I go to the picket before school sometimes
        and when Rafa is there.
Papá doesn't say so outright,
        but I can tell he is still sour
about my union card
        because he still doesn't invite me
to the picket with them.

Despite the growing cold
        of the misty mornings
of fall that surrounds us
        and enters through

my thin blue sweater,
   I am warmed by the picket.

I am warmed by the people,
    by their chants,
    by their voices,
    by their wishes
for things to be fair.

I add my raspy shouts,

   "Que viva la causa! ¡Que viva la huelga!"

But it isn't enough,
   so I add a rolling thunder sound
with my feet and hands
   to join everyone's hope
that one day soon
   our people will win.

JANITOR JOB

Rafa takes Mamá
to the clinic so often,
they offer him a job.

To clean up after the nurses,
the doctor, and Doña Serafina, who now
works there because farmworkers trust her.

Papá doesn't say no to Rafa
taking the job because
he'd still be working for la causa.

I think Papá secretly knows
being close to the clinic
might get Mamá more of the help she needs.

Even if it means
Rafa can't be with him
on the picket.

Rafa tells me and Concha
he'll watch closely and take mental notes
on how they take care of their patients.

"One day, it could come in handy," he says, and shrugs
his shoulders. "Maybe one day, I could be a nurse."

His eyes shine as he says so.
I hope Papá's rules won't stop him
from seeing it through.

AFTER-SCHOOL COMMOTION

After school sometimes
Leonor and I go to the picket line
if we can get a ride.
I try to stay away
from Papá's picket
now that Rafa's at work.

> "Stick with Leonor, like chicles andantes," Mamá says,
> when I get her permission to go.

Today, Leonor's tito Philip takes us
to a picket close to Delano city.
We arrive to an uproar
> of people yelling and laughing
> gathered in a big crowd.

Leonor asks a woman standing
near the back what's happening.

> "It's El Teatro Campesino. They're putting on a show."

We move in a zigzag trying
to get a view of the commotion.
My mind is a curious tangle
over what it might be.

When we break into a clearing
what I see takes me in an instant
> to the carpa.
But there is no tent,
there is no ringmaster, no lights.

Something brighter
        shines on the back of a pickup truck
        used as a stage,
        with actors.

(A pig-masked man with a sign around his neck that reads "Mr. Marrano")
MR. MARRANO: "Look here, dirty little grape pickers, I
mean no harm when I exploit you. I only want to grow
and sell my grapes at market and make
more money than you can ever dream of."
(He turns around and laughs mockingly.)

The audience around me boos at him as if on cue.

(A farmworker with a sign around his neck that says "Campesino" steps up to Mr. Marrano)
CAMPESINO: If you want us to work, Mr. Marrano, the
union has one or two demands.

MR. MARRANO: "Ha! Never mind that. Why don't you get
to picking my grapes as you are told!" *(Mr. Marrano
pretends to eat grapes one by one and laughs)*

*(Campesino shoves a scroll of paper in front of Mr.
Marrano)*
CAMPESINO: "Of course! Just sign this itsy-witsy con-
tract and we can all get back to work." *(The scroll of
paper unfurls, touches the ground, and keeps rolling.)*

A full-blown giggle
        grows inside me
                and I ride a shooting star
                        of laughter.

                              I join Leonor, who
                folds over hysterically
        along with
the crowd.

This is not the carpa,
        but it is close.
It's warm, familiar, funny!

My daydreams and la causa
have come together to give me
        a new thing
        to dream
        and be
        someday.

EL TEATRO CAMPESINO

We learn from a man at the picket,

El Teatro Campesino is a theater
    of farmworkers
    like us.

They do skits about our lucha
    to teach
    la gente.

They mock the growers
    for fun.

Their stages are flatbeds or dirt beds,
    any place is fine.

They are poor
    like us.

They belong to the union
    to help la causa.

Only men are actors.
    Their leader is
    Luis Valdez.

Their voices are loud
    and wild
    un. like. mine.

DO I DARE?

                Leonor hangs on my shoulder,
        still laughing, but I am
in a trance.

When they're done, I approach an actor
        with deep friendly dimples
                who someone called Agustín.

I want to ask him how
        I can join El Teatro Campesino,
                but my voice betrays me.

My vocal cords are wrapped
        in the wasp's nest of my rasp
        and the nerve to speak.

Agustín smiles at me but looks away
        quickly because
        I don't say anything.

I slip on the mud of my mind
        without a daydream
        without a voice
        motionless against miles
        of unharvested vineyards
        holding hostage
        all of my one-day dreams.

UP TO ME

Leonor sees me crumble
at not being able to speak.
She comes to me
with a half a smile
looking to lift
one in me.

"I . . . I could . . . I couldn't ask him my question," I say.

She shoves my arm gently.

"It's okay! What'd you want to ask him, anyway?"

I share with Leonor
about losing my voice
to the wind in the Imperial Valley,
about the carpa,
about wanting to be a ringmaster,
and how similar El Teatro is to the carpa,
and she gets it.

"Oh, it's your dream! Like how I want to be a pilot?" She
says, "Maybe there's a way to make it happen! We're
gonna have to find out."

Leonor brings me
strength like Concha
though I know it's up to me
to get my real voice back
if I ever want to join.

ACTOS

Leonor and I find out
El Teatro rehearses
near the NFWA offices.
We scheme to get a ride the next day after school.

We get there and find
       Agustín strumming a guitar,
       and a man with a mustache
       like a thick hairy caterpillar
       above his top lip
trying to convince a group of men
to join El Teatro.

       "Our job is to make statements through actos, these
       small skits will show people the fact that there is a
       strike going on right now," the man says.

       "But what if they don't get it, Luis?" another young man
       says.

       "They will. The point is to put the grower on stage,
       make fun of him, so others will know what he is like."

The mustached man is the leader
we saw the other day, Luis Valdez.
His voice is like
the low roar of an engine,
strong and firm.

       "But I don't know how to act, much less read," an older
       man says.

"This is El Teatro Campesino! A theater for the people
and by the people. Everyone here is welcome and
everyone here is an actor. You've lived these experiences.
No one knows them better than you," Luis says.

The words "everyone is welcome"
        land lightly
                inside my lungs,
                        expands them and fills them
                                with the courage to speak up.

I raise my hand
but Luis and Agustín don't see me.
Leonor turns to me
with a puzzled look.
She mouths,

        "What are you doing, Lula?"

I nod my head as if to tell her
        she will have to wait and see.
                I raise my hand higher.

But they still don't see
a small girl like me.
Luis claps his hands quickly
and says,

        "All right, gentlemen. Let's get to work!"

IF . . .

If I had a real voice.
If I were not a kid.
If I were not a girl.

Would they have let me in?

REHEARSALS

When we can, Leonor and I return
to watch El Teatro rehearse in Delano
or watch them perform wherever they are.

El Teatro is like magic for the strike.
        They help bring workers out of the fields.
        They make even the most stubborn scabs
        understand through music,
        through laughter, and poking fun,
        the need for us to be successful.

Papá and Mamá don't know
I've been attending rehearsals
after school with Leonor.
They think we're picketing the farms.

When we do go to Delano,
Leonor and I catch a bus ride back
to our labor camp with Concha.
I ask Concha if I should tell Papá
about wanting to be in El Teatro.

        "What for? And risk him getting mad at you? You aren't
        a part of El Teatro anyway," she says, frowning.

She's right, but she
doesn't have to rub it in.

MAMÁ'S BEANS

Mamá praises the morning sun
when she thanks God for another day.

I love to see her up in the mornings
making food again,
though she moves with a delicate pace,
as if touching the earth
hurts her.

She is growing back into herself
with help from the clinic and Rafa.
Slowly healing into December.

I feel lucky that because of the strike
she doesn't have to go to the fields
but can stay home to heal,
and can do as she is doing now
sorting and cleaning beans
on her apron on her lap.

Mamá glides her open hand
across the beans, looking for rocks.
She nods, and hums a bolero she loves.

She pushes on, though we don't
have all of her test results back
and we fuss over helping her.

She sighs often yet still
offers us a smile to shoo off the worry
we have over her.

IMPROVISATION

Leonor and I blend into
a group of other onlookers
as El Teatro rehearses.

El Teatro practices "improvisation"
      —things they make up
            straight from their brains.

This is my favorite part
of how El Teatro works.
Luis comes to the group
      with an idea for an acto
      and he helps the actors make up the lines.

      "What we are doing here is creation. Creation for el
      movimiento." Luis says to the actors. "To improvise, you
      have to tap into the character, Mr. Fuchiface, Mr. Gio-
      gordo, the sheriff—any of them. And now think about
      how that character might feel deep inside, and say the
      first silly thing that comes to your mind."

I follow along and think
      of a million silly things to say
that I don't say.

I practice improvisation
      under my breath.

OUTLAWED

The next morning Leonor comes to our barrack, crying.

> Her mamá, Señora De la Cruz
> has been arrested
> on the picket.
>
> She said the Delano County Sheriff
> has made it against the law
> to say "huelga" in public.

The word for strike in Spanish
> is so powerful,
> the growers don't have
> another way to fight us
> but to bribe the police
> to take away our right
> to speak out.

> The union leaders asked
> some of the members
> to go against the police
> and say it anyway.
> Señora De la Cruz, Helen Chávez,
> Esther Urunday, from the membership
> office and thirty-seven other mothers,
> stepped up to disobey
> the unfair law.

Now they are all in prison
> and Leonor wants my help
> to get her mamá out.

A SOFT PLACE

Leonor hugs me tightly
and sobs into my shoulder.

I really don't know
what I can do.

Right now, I am grateful
to be a soft place
for her cries to land.

AIN'T AFRAID OF NO JAIL

The next day, we ride Leonor's truck
loaded with kids from our camp,
headed for the jail in Delano.

Many of their mamás
have also been arrested.
The rest of us come
in solidarity.

No one is crying.
I can tell some of them
are swallowing their fear.

No one knows when
their parents will be free,
but the union has a plan.

When we arrive to the jailhouse,
there are reporters shoving microphones
and cameras in our faces.

Leonor's dad, Mr. De la Cruz,
clears the way for his truck load
to join a crowd of other kids
picketing the jail.

For the first time,
the kids protesting
with picket signs
and rising voices
outnumber the grown-ups.

We can't say "huelga,"
but we shout,

> "We ain't afraid of no jail!
> We want our mamis!
> We ain't afraid of no jail!
> We want our mamis!"

It feels right to be here with Leonor,
though I'm straining to be heard.

The orange-yellow mist
of my voice folds
into the chanting
of seventy-six kids
all wanting for justice
to be done.

FREE

Our protest helped!

On the third day,
with the news coverage
and the bail paid by donations,
they let the prisoners
                              go free
and Señora De la Cruz
comes home
to Leonor.

TO EL TEATRO

Leonor and me go back
to El Teatro rehearsals
again and again by catching rides
from everyone she knows
until Leonor says,

> "Lula, I don't want to discourage you, but I don't think
> they'll let any kid into their group."

> "One day, it'll happen. Maybe if we make ourselves useful?"

> "But they barely notice we're here. Besides, it looks like it's
> a men-only thing."

She's right, we are as invisible as a backdrop,
though I hate to admit it.
> We hang around El Teatro
> with a swarm of actors' children
> who look on and play tag
> while their fathers rehearse.

I don't play with the others,
like Leonor does.

Instead, I play out the actos in my mind
and memorize the songs
Agustín and Luis make up for the movement.

"Viva la huelga en el fiel.
> Viva la causa en la historiaaaa.
> La raza llena de gloriaaaa,
> la victoria va cumplir."

Leonor nudges me with her elbow
as if hoping I'll agree with her,
but I'm not giving up.

Without Leonor, I'd have to figure out
a way to get to rehearsals
after school by myself.

OUT

Later that day, when Concha, Leonor, and I
get off the bus from Delano,
> we find Mamá sitting
>> at the labor camp's roadside
>> with the babies
>> and the few belongings we have.

>> There is a row of families
>> waiting and lining the road
>> with their belongings too.
>> While others are piling
>>> their things
>>>> onto trucks and leaving.

Martín squirms in Mamá's arms
> while Gabi plays in the dirt.
>> Mamá's lips are cracked,
>>> the lines on her forehead
>> are creased like a washboard.

"Mamá, ¿qué pasó? Why are you all here?" I ask.

"The growers kicked all of the strikers out of the barracks," she says, shaking slightly, I'm not sure if from
susto or from her sickness.

Concha gasps. "They have no right! We pay rent!"

"What could I do when they kicked us out at gunpoint!?
They said their barracks were reserved for people who
want to work. They are trying to punish us for striking,
for being a part of the union."

At hearing this,
        Leonor rushes away
to find her family.

        "Where will we go, Mamá?" I ask. A flood of nerves
        courses through me.

Papá and Rafa have no idea
        what's happened.

                They won't be home till later.

                        A home we no longer have.

BACKUP

Delano's December cold has no mercy
       as night falls.

     "We've got to get to the offices in Delano, even if we
     have to walk," Concha says, though I don't know what
     good that would do.

We gather as much as we can into
             our hands and arms but
                       it is no use, we need the whole family
                       here to be able to carry our things.

We'll have to wait, but the darkness grows around us.
Leonor's family left in their packed pickup truck.
I don't know where they are going.

Just then, an old bus pulls up beside us.
     When the door opens,
          Dolores Huerta comes out.

Luckily, Concha now knows Dolores
because of her job as after-school secretary,
and so Dolores approaches us first.

     "I can't believe the heartlessness of these growers," Do-
     lores says to us while shaking her head. "We got calls
     that they'd evicted people, so we are fitting as many as
     we can into this bus and making rounds. We'll figure
     out what we are going to do about housing our families."

My eyes water in relief.
Dolores is not going to let us down.

BARRACKLESS

We board the bus
and wait for others to load in.

Concha buries
her head in her hands
and cries.

I am on the verge too
when Mamá pleads with us,

"Be strong, mis amores. The growers will not have the
last word."

I see my old Mamá for a moment
not as sick as she's been
but strong and brave for us.

She says the barracks
are not a home anyway,
they're only a shell.

She says,

"Remember, mi'jas. We are migrant farmworkers.
Like seeds, we carry home in our bodies. Home is
where we grow it, together."

FILIPINO COMMUNITY HALL SHELTER

When we finally reunite in Delano
with Papá and Rafa, Papá is fuming.

The union hall is filled with evicted families
each making beds by laying blankets on the floor.

Concha has gone to the NFWA offices
to work on finding us another place to stay.

I see Leonor and her family and I'm so relieved,
but I don't visit her so as not to leave Mamá.

Papá bangs his fist into his hand.

> "Malditos. Makes me want to burn down their fields," he
> says.

A fellow striker overhears Papá,

> "No, mi hermano. That's not how we fight. We've got to
> stay calm and nonviolent. That's how we will overcome."

Papá looks embarrassed because that man
pointed out his short fuse.

> "Let's go to the mess hall and get some food," Papá says,
> trying to brush off his anger.

Before we leave, Leonor and I exchange worried eyes,
but all we can do is wave from a distance for now.

IN THE STRUGGLE

From the stage, Gil Padilla gets the attention
of the crowd of uncertain farmworker families
      shoulders drooped
      heads lowered
      eating in the mess hall.

      "Compañeros, thank you for your atención. It is my
      honor to present to you one of our fearless leaders, a
      great man, Larry Itliong of the AWOC-AFLCIO, who is
      here to give a few words."

Larry Itliong steps up to the podium,
his face wearing both
      a soothing kindness like Mamá's
      and the strength of granite.

He begins to address people in English
sprinkled with a few words I've heard
Leonor say is Tagalog.

      "Magandang gabi. Welcome to Filipino Hall. For years,
      the growers have been pitting us against one
      another. Filipino crews against Mexican crews. Negro
      crews against Arab crews. I want to let you know that
      you have a home here at Filipino Hall, a hall built for
      the Filipinos who have been working these fields for
      decades. We are doing something new by coming to-
      gether. That's what makes our fight different.
      We are not afraid of the growers though they can be
      nasty. When they evict strikers, no matter if you are
      Filipino, Mexican, Arab, Negro, or Oakie, we will be
      there to catch you when you fall. This is what this place

is for. For this struggle. For us to gather, to break bread, to think about how we are going make the growers fold and give us the wages we deserve. Please make yourselves at home. We are fighting this arm in arm and trust that we will win in the end!"

I turn to see that Leonor and her family
are now sitting a few tables
over from us.

When Larry Itliong is done,
Leonor's dad, Mr. De La Cruz,
shoots up to standing like a
rocket
alongside other Filipinos
roaring with applause.

Leonor wraps her arms
around her father
and squeezes her eyes shut.

Their smiles are a starlit sky
filled with light
that shines on us all.

PAPÁ'S CESAR

Gil Padilla approaches the podium
and his hearty clap pours into the mic.
Between excited breaths, Gil thanks Larry and says,

> "It is equally an honor to introduce you to our other leader
> in this lucha, president of the NFWA, Cesar Chávez!" Gil,
> bows his head and moves his turned-up hand to Cesar,
> who comes up to the podium with a shy smile and speaks.

> "Brothers and sisters, we are with you. It isn't fair that
> the growers have thrown you out of their barracks. We
> are grateful to sister Dolores Huerta, who was able to
> organize transportation to bring some of you here. We
> are doing all we can to find everyone housing. In the
> meantime, we cannot lose faith. This action by the
> growers means they are feeling the pressure of our
> strike. We are going to get fair wages and dignity in the
> fields. It is going to change but we must persevere with
> every challenge and respond with nonviolent actions."

I turn to see Papá watch Cesar speak
and he looks even more inspired than in the carpa.
I look closer and I see a reflection.
> They could be brothers
> with their reddish-brown skin,
> lean, slightly hooked nose,
> thick, deep black hair.

Cesar's eyes speak
the language of peace and nonviolence,
one that Papá's still learning
but that has already changed
Papá for the better.

SOLIDARIDAD

After Larry Itliong and Cesar Chávez,
Agustín from El Teatro
takes the microphone
and launches into a song
I know from rehearsals
and the picket line.

> "Solidaridad pa' siempre,
> Solidaridad pa' siempre,
> Solidaridad pa' siempre.
> ¡Que viva nuestra union!"

Papá begins to sing.
Mamá and Rafa join too.
Gabi babbles the words,
while Martín bounces to the music
in Mamá's arms.

I've never sung the words
solidarity forever out loud
but I try anyway knowing
that my voice will wash into
the many voices of hope
singing in a chorus.

SUN RAYS

Concha moved
     a mountain
     to find us a place!

She says it's a rental in Delano
not too far from the NFWA offices.
Donations from the Quakers
are helping us pay for it.

It has   running water,
       electricity, a refrigerator, a stove,
       its own bathroom,
       and two actual bedrooms!

Though we can't move in
for another two days.

     Meanwhile, we make the best of being
     here in the Filipino Community Hall turned shelter
     because we are in the heart of the movement.
     No one here is mean, or rude
     even though we're sleeping piled up like pebbles.

Plus, I don't need to find a ride
to see El Teatro Campesino rehearse
because their rehearsals are right here.

     I don't miss going to school because we are in the
     thick of la causa. I only miss the stars over the bar-
     racks at night and the fields opening like sun rays
     around us.

WHILE WE WAIT

Mamá gathers with other mothers, compañeras,
        to cook food while they talk about the strike
        and what they might do to help.

Papá keeps going to the picket line,
Rafa goes to his janitor job,
and Concha to Delano High.

I've got nowhere to go and neither does Leonor
        until we can transfer
        to Delano Middle School.

So, I invite Leonor to scavenge
        for furniture or things we can put inside
        our new casita when we get it.

But mostly, I try to follow El Teatro
        wherever they go.

A SURPRISE VISIT

Leonor and I go to see Rafa at the clinic,
which is a mobile home
parked in an empty lot.

People wait beneath
a little wood shade structure
they built out front.

As we approach the door
Rafa comes out holding
a broom and dust pan in his hands.

> "Hey, hermanita! Hey, Leonor! What're you
> two doing here?" he says with a smile so big
> it makes his eyes squint.

> "I hope it's okay. I've just never seen where
> you work," I say.

Rafa brings us inside to meet
the nurses, Helen and Mary,
and Doña Serafina.
We don't meet the doctor because
he's only there on the weekends.

The farmworker flag
hangs right above a desk.
I take a deep breath,
so glad to finally see the place
that's making Mamá well.

DOÑA SERAFINA TEA

Doña Serafina says goodbye
to a patient before she turns to us
and says,

> "This has to be your sister, Rafa. She's got
> your same thick eyelashes!" She taps my arm
> gently and she smiles at Leonor.

> "Mucho gusto, Señora. Thank you for helping
> my mother feel better," I say shyly.

Doña Serafina raises one eyebrow
and asks me why my voice
is so hoarse.

She must have seen
my frozen expression and says,

> "No matter, mi'ja Tell me, does it hurt you?"

I look over to Rafa,
who nods quickly
as if letting me know
it's okay to confide in her.

I swallow hard and say,

> "It doesn't hurt, but it just doesn't work like it used to."

> "Let me see. Can you open your mouth for me
> to look inside?" she asks.

"Go on, Lula. Let her check you," Rafa says.

Doña Serafina grins
after she inspects my throat and says,

> "Mm-hmm. Your vocal cords and throat look
> irritated. You didn't happen to be with your
> mamá when they sprayed the fields?" she
> says as she lifts my chin up toward her face to
> look at my eyes.

I flash back to the remolino again
and nod in silence.

> "Claro, it makes sense. But don't worry, mi'ja.
> This is nothing a good salvia and dried apple
> tea can't fix."

Leonor puts a happy arm
over my shoulders
when we walk away.

I hold a brown paper bag
filled with Doña Serafina's herbs.
I recognize the sage because
it grows wild in the fields
where I forage.

I hold the onto the belief
that drinking in their healing
will help bring back my voice.

"LAS DOS CARAS DEL PATRONCITO."

I watch El Teatro's next rehearsal
        as quietly
as a waiting seed.

Luis sets up a new idea:
        to show how the bosses
        double-cross everyone.

The acto has three characters:

LITTLE BOSS OR "PATRONCITO": A two-faced boss *(wears a mask that is half pig)*

ESQUIROL: A scab brought in from Mexico to break the strike

LA JURA: A police officer who is on the side of the boss.

Luis sets up the scene:

"The 'patroncito' is very friendly with his scab at first but then slowly reveals his pig face as he works him hard and unfairly. By the time the scab realizes he has been tricked, he protests. He gets dragged away by the Sherriff, screaming for help from Cesar Chávez and the union!"

The men get to improvising
and happiness pops in me to watch them
spin the story into life and laughter.

SPROUTING

Luis Valdez asks
a group of kids
running around,

"Are there any volunteers with good penmanship?"

I look around.
The kids don't hear him.

I gulp. My swallow feels
like a lump of clay in my throat.

I raise my hand, slowly.
In case he ignores me again.

But then I think
about how Mamá
asked for us to be brave
and how Dolores
is not afraid of anyone,
not the growers,
and not Papá.
So, I let my arm
shoot up fast.

And he *sees* me!

He calls me to him
with his pointed finger.

"You're sure you can write English and Spanish and
have good penmanship?" he questions me.

I nod excitedly.

"Yes, sir," I say, without much of a rasp at all!

"Good, first you need to find some strong pieces of cardboard about this big, you see?" He shows me another
sign. "Then you'll have to make a sign for each of these
characters: 'EL PATRONCITO' for the little boss, 'LA JURA'
for the security guard, 'ESQUIROL' for the scab. Got
that?"

I can hardly believe it.
I'm doing a job for El Teatro!

When I am done
and I show
him the signs,
he tells me,

"Good job, kid! Though we don't use props as a rule, you
can make signs for El Teatro Campesino anytime, if
you're up for it."

"Thank you," I say, and then I clear my throat and ask,
"Is this an official job?"

"I wouldn't go that far. But keep at it and we'll see how it
goes," Luis says, and taps me softly on the shoulder.

Though it isn't
what I want exactly,
it's getting closer.

My body sways
     in circles of joy
          as I walk back
               to the shelter.

I'm not sure if it was
Doña Serafina's tea
or if it was me
who brought back my voice.

I can't wait to tell
my siblings and Mamá.

At this moment,
     my dream
          feels as if
               it is sprouting
                    and breaking
                        through earth
                            softened by rain.

ROSE HUGS

I huddle with
my siblings and Mamá
at the union hall shelter
in the evening.

Before we can say a word,
Rafa holds up a paper from the clinic
and reads us Mamá's skin test results,

    "Mamá's *negative* for cancer!"

We all lean into Mamá
like petals into a rose.

Our hugs fold into a tight
loving bud and then expand
as our tears turn from relief to laughter.

I curl into Mamá's
arm and tell her,

    "Mamá, I am so happy you're going to be okay."

    "Me too, Lulita. Thank God for all of you and
    the strike."

BLOOMING NEWS

"I also have some good news," Concha says. "I met all the
fall deadlines and submitted ten applications to college!"

"When will you know if you got in?" Rafa asks.

"I gave the NFWA offices' address and I'll know if I'm
accepted early next year."

We wrap her in more hugs and congratulations.

Then Rafa tells us,

"The doctor asked me if I wanted to be a nurse's apprentice
at the clinic! With Doña Serafina there, now I will be
training in herbs and healing the Mexican way and the
doctor's way too."

With all the goodness,
I have the courage to finally share
about being the *almost* sign maker
for El Teatro Campesino.

I speak it in a voice
without a rasp, without a whisper, without a crack.

Mamá hugs me when I finish
and she says,

"There's my Lula's voice I've missed so much!" She holds
her cheek wet from tears against mine and tops it with
a kiss.

WAKING

My voice is waking up
      from a long,
            long,
                  sleep.

I am less
      afraid
          to speak.

NOT NOW

Perhaps it is better, Mamá says,
to not tell Papá just yet.

Concha's news.
Rafa's news.
My news.

>"He's sensitive to those kinds of things," Mamá says.

>"Or machista," Concha says and puts two fists on her hips.

>"What do you mean?" Mamá asks.

>"Macho, Mamá. You know. He expects girls and women to
>only be one way and not equal to men," Concha says.

>"Yeah! It's why he won't listen to Dolores Huerta and
>doesn't want Concha to go to college or for Concha
>and me to go to the picket," I say.

>"But it's also that he'll think that I can't be a nurse
>because I'm a boy," Rafa adds.

Mamá stops to consider
what we say.
She looks at us quietly,
lifts her hand to rub her temple
and says,

>"Quizás, that's true. But it is the only Papá you have and
>we need to find a way for him to understand, por las
>buenas."

It makes me suddenly sad
that we have to keep
our happiness from Papá
because it will make him mad.

"For now, we can tell him that I don't have cancer. The
rest of our news will have to wait." Mamá nods her
head as if hoping we will agree with her.

Our Papá is too machista
to handle any more.

OUR NEW HOUSE

Our new house
>>> is older and more chipped
>>> than the labor camp school,
>>> but it's more of a home
>>> than we have ever had.

Our new house
>>> has a crooked screen door,
>>> a small yard with quelites, sage, an apple tree,
>>> where Mamá wants to grow more food
>>> and let the babies play.

Our new house
>>> has a flush toilet, a shower,
>>> water running from the faucets,
>>> and windows where the busy bustle
>>> of Delano peppered with people
>>> comes into view.

Our new house
>>> sits in a neighborhood
>>> so different from any labor camp
>>> we've ever lived, with sidewalks
>>> and streets, and neighbors
>>> who don't all work the fields.

Our new house
>>> is strange and broken a little around the edges
>>> but we don't mind; it's so much better than before.
>>> It's a new shell, where we *will* grow.

BIG SKY MOVES

It doesn't take much for us
to move into our new place in Delano city
because we've got little to move.

We set up a few chairs
I found on the street
while scavenging with Leonor
and we string up our hammocks
so we don't have to sleep on the floor.

It's different than hanging beneath the trees
and gazing at the star-filled sky
but now I understand why Mamá said
it's cozier when we're together.

Mamá is stunned
when las compañeras
show up with a truckload of donations:
food, hand-me-down clothes, shoes for us all,
a couch, a table, and more chairs.

A storm is clearing.

We all have jobs:
School. The clinic. The strike.
To get better. To play and be a baby.
Maybe, El Teatro.

We *have* one another
under this old roof,
under a cloudless sky.

LEONOR'S FAMILY

I look for Leonor at the union hall
and she tells me her family
found a place to live
only two blocks away.

We'll still be neighbors!
We'll both be at the same school!

Her family had lived
in the chinche barracks
for as long as Leonor could remember
because of her dad's year-round job.
But the strike ended that,
and the alliance helped them
into what they have now
just like us.

Leonor says,

> "Can you believe? A flush toilet in the house!"

We laugh at the mention of toilets.
But then we both stop suddenly,
and my heart bunches into a knot
to realize that our families
never had one before.

BACK TO ME

Delano Middle School
isn't like labor camp schools.
There are *so* many kids.

They've got real classrooms,
an auditorium, a lunchroom, lockers,
and nothing is broken.

Though it's all a little awkward,
Leonor and I pick up
right where we left off.

She knows some of the kids
because she doesn't forget names
and because she doesn't wait to meet people.

We avoid meeting the kids
with nice clothes and girls with too much makeup
because we think they might be growers' kids.

And because I'm always
right by her,
some know *me*.

Once, we imitate El Teatro during lunchtime
and a couple kids gather around
to see the chisme.

This time, they not only
watch Leonor's fast engine mouth
but they hear me try to sing with her.

"El picket sign, el picket sign.
Lo llevo por todo el día.
El picket sign, el picket sign.
It's with me all day looooong!"

An audience of two
hears my voice beginning
to come back to me.

PAPÁ MIGHT

A few nights later, El Teatro is set to perform
at a rally at the Filipino Community Hall
and I've *got* to be there
to see them and the signs
I made for the troupe.

> I come with Leonor and see Concha is among
> the organizers, setting out folding chairs,
> greeting people and helping them find a seat.

I'm worried to see Papá arrive;
he looks anxious
holding his folded arms to his chest.

> If Concha is right, he might get angry
> at me for getting involved.

But I *should* be allowed
to participate in the struggle,
as a card-carrying striker,
and as a helper for El Teatro.

> I'm strong enough and ready to tell him
> but I hold back because I promised Mamá
> we wouldn't share our news yet.

I plant my feet firmly
on the wood floor,
ball my hands into fists,
and brace myself
for what Papá might say.

BREAK A LEG!

I sit by the actors,
       holding everything in a basket:
       the pig-faced mask, the signs I made,
       a sheriff's badge.

Papá lifts his head at me as if asking, "What's going on?"

I look right at him and just wave, hoping my happy face will make him back off.

But then Luis asks us to come outside to get ready for the performance. They are about to go on.

When I hand out the signs, I say to them,

       "Break a leg!"

Just like they said we should do when we wish an actor good luck.

I slip back into the audience when the lights are out
       and I am swept into
       the sunshine of El Teatro's story
       of the two-faced boss
       and a forever message
       that the struggle will succeed.

Papá must have gotten lost in El Teatro's show too,
       because he didn't look my way again
       and doesn't ask me anything at home.

A SOFTENING

I slide out of my hammock
      the next morning when I hear
Mamá and Papá in the kitchen,
      whispering.
I know it's about us because I hear our names
      Concha, Rafa, Lula, Gabi, Martín,
shuffled between their quiet talking.

I enter the room slowly
      and Mamá says, "Buenos días, hija."
Her face, a bright spot
      in the shade of the cold morning.

      "Lula, Papá wants you to go with him to the picket today."

Mamá notices the terrain
      of my face is unsettled
with what she's said.

      "I . . . I . . ." I start but pause.

Papá catches
      my stuttering
with his soft words.

      "I could really use a translator out on the picket, now
      that Rafa's at his janitor's job."

      "Si, Papá. I'd really love that," I answer.

Disbelief and excitement
whirring like wind in my heart.

DRINK-FREE ALLIANCE

When Papá gets in the shower
before we leave,
Mama tells me
Papá has promised
not to drink anymore.

Cesar said he didn't want
any drunks in the movement
squandering their money,
and so Papá had to make a vow.

> "It's been months since he's had a drink," she says,
> shaking her head slowly.

Happy tears twirl
in my eyes because
it explains why
my drink-free Papá
is inviting me to go.

But also, what else
is he willing to allow
                    now that he's sober?

WE'RE LOSING SUPPORT

Outside donations aren't
coming in as fast as when
we started the strike
six months ago.

The cold spreads through
January and into February
chilling more than the crops
because the alliance is in trouble.

Some of the strikers have
gone back to the fields
and it's hurting us.

The picket line is getting
more violent and just yesterday
the police beat two strikers, a man and a woman,
who stood in front of buses filled with braceros
    —scabs brought from Mexico.
The police beat the strikers black and blue
and didn't care if their kids
were watching.

Dolores, Larry, and Cesar
take turns to ask us to hold on,
to not break the strike.
No matter what comes,
we must be true to our vow
to remain nonviolent.

AROUND OUR TABLE

We sit for dinner
      around our table
like a tightly wound leaf
      before it unfurls.

Papá is more serious
      than we've seen him lately,
      though he still isn't drinking.

We can't help talk about
      the strike's troubles.

      "So what are we going to do now that people are
      leaving the strike?" Rafa asks.

      "The leadership is forming a plan. They want to get
      through the end of February and into the spring, when
      the growers will need us again, to lay on the biggest
      pressure," Papá says. His worries speak loudly on his face.

      "I'm so thankful Concha helped us find this house. We
      have a nice warm heater!" Mamá says, trying to lighten
      the mood.

      "When she graduates college, she'll move us to an even
      better one than this!" I say, suddenly realizing I prob-
      ably shouldn't have.

I wince a bit
      and when I open my eyes,
Papá is going

from me to Concha,
          from Concha to Mamá,
looking for meaning.

"No me digas that you still have those pipe dreams fill-
ing your head, Concha. And you're telling them to your
sister?" Papá's voice rises.

"Papá," Rafa interrupts, "it's not what you think. It's only
a silly schoolgirl dream. Concha's not going anywhere."
But then he says to me through gritted teeth, "Ay, big
mouth."

"I am not a big mouth for telling the truth!" I yell at him.

"Wait a minute. What truth? What do you know that I
don't, Rafa? Concha?" He pushes for answers.

Concha glares at me,
          then puts her hands
on the table and calmly says,

          "I applied to ten different colleges."

The room is thick with silence.

          "And there's more, Papá," Concha says.

Rafa looks at Concha,
          shakes his head telling
her to stop talking, but
          Concha continues,

          "Rafa is now—"

"I'm now a nurse's apprentice at the clinic!" Rafa beats
her to it and purses his lips at us. Then he says,

"And Lula is being a metiche with El Teatro Campesino."

I am so mad at Rafa
but madder at Papá
        for making it so we
we have to hide.

I fling Papá's contradictions at him.

"Why should we keep from doing what we love
because you say so, Papá? How can we be fighting for
justice for our people when there is no justice in our
own family?"

THRASHING LEAVES

Papá's hurt feelings
            hurl around the room
         like leaves caught in
wicked Santa Ana winds.

He bangs on the table with one of his fists.
            The impact makes us jump.

     "You are all malcriados! How dare you take liberties like
     that? College is no place for a farmworker's daughter."
     He points at Concha and then thuds his chest with an
     open palm and says, "My son will not do a woman's job."
     Then he turns to me and says, "And you, escuincla, that
     troupe is for men. Teatro is no place for decent women!"

     "Pero Papá!" Concha begins to reason, but Papá lands his
     open hands on the table.

     "Viejo, ¡basta!" Mamá's voice breaks the reverberation.
     "Our children don't deserve this. They are trying to be
     of service. These are the things that make them happy.
     They want . . ." Mamá pauses. "I want them to find their
     own paths."

With one quick movement,
         Papá unbuckles and removes his belt,
making it slap against itself like a whip.

Gabi and Martín wail at the sound.

Mamá puts her arms to his chest and pleads,

"¡Por favor, no!" But he slides her arms away with the back of his arm.

"There will be no college!" He smacks the table with his belt, then says, "No clinic!" and slaps it again, and then says, "AND no teatro!" With one final smack, he heaves, he's hit the table so hard. "Aquí mando yo, and I decide how you live your lives."

His fury sends us into silence.
I am relieved he wasn't drunk
and didn't turn the belt on us.

Papá walks out of the room,
          a tornado lifting up every field,
tree, and leaf,
          and imploding on itself.

Dried leaves turn into a fog
          of soot so thick,
it crashes against our dreams.

RETREAT

We each retreat
        into ourselves
        to the place of seeds
        where there is only silence,
        to a ground so dark,
                absent of sun.

What do we a call a thing
        that doesn't allow
        a seed to grow?

Do we call it frost?

Winter?

Poison?

Papá?

FRUTA

Every time we sit at a table at night or in the morning
to enjoy the fruits and grain and vegetables from our
good Earth, remember that they come from the work
of men and women and children who have been
exploited for generations . . .
—Cesar Chávez

WE OBEY PAPÁ

In the quiet,
I am safe from Papá's winter
because now spring opens into March.

In the quiet,
I count blessings with no room
to be ungrateful, malcriada.

In the quiet,
Mamá doesn't have cancer,
though she feels sick again.

In the quiet,
Concha will not leave
any of us.

In the quiet,
Rafa went back to being a janitor;
at least he has a job.

In the quiet,
the alliance needs our help
more than ever.

In the quiet,
Leonor and I
sneak to pickets and rehearsals.

In the quiet,
I don't have a voice
but I do.

                              I do.

BIG CALLING

When she gets home,
Concha drops her things
on the couch while she reads
yet another rejection letter.

It's almost as if
the colleges she applied to
are in cahoots with Papá
to not let her go.

I can tell it is a rejection
by the way she tears
the envelope in two
and rushes to say,

"The leadership is calling the biggest meeting of farmworkers yet!"

"I'm sorry, Concha," I say because I know it hurts her.
"You've still got a few more to hear from, right?"

"Never mind that, Lulita." Concha shakes her head,
though the disappointment is painted on her face.

She tells me how the leaders
are planning a strong action
something drastic, to bring
more attention to la causa.

"You remember President Kennedy, the one who was
killed a couple of years ago? Well, his brother Bobby,

who's a senator, is coming for a congressional meeting
on migration," Concha says.

"What's that have to do with our grape strike?" I ask.

"So many migrants are farmworkers. It ties right in."

Concha also explains the alliance is going
to take advantage of the news stations
that will be here to cover it.

The meeting is in a couple of weeks.
Everyone's getting ready to mobilize.
They aren't saying what it will look like.

No matter, I can feel this is going to be
a big moment for the movement
and I wonder what El Teatro will do.

PILGRIMAGE

> I sneak away
> to the next teatro rehearsal.
> Everyone is abuzz over
> the upcoming action;
> they fly around like June bugs
> near the light.

I learn that the action the alliance has decided
is a 300-mile pilgrimage to Sacramento,
but for now it's a secret from the press.
It's everyone's responsibility
to keep it that way until it is announced.

> The pilgrimage will pass through
> every farming town, looking for support for the strike.
> Until they reach the governor's office in the capitol.
> All to bring national attention to the fight
> of the farmworkers.

Every man, woman, and child are welcome
to come on the peaceful march, they said.
It's a long way to go, but,

"El Teatro Campesino will be there to lift spirits with
actos and canciones!" Agustín sings loudly while he
strums his guitar.

"That's a lot of actos, so we better get to brainstorming!"
Luis says.

PEQUEÑA

Agustín sees me standing by the door,
and motions me to come closer.

> "Let's see, pequeña, you've been here enough that you
> know this song by now, right?" he says and begins to
> play "Niños Campesinos," their song for farmworker kids.

A flutter forms in my chest
but I shake it off and begin
to sing along with him,

> "El sol calienta ranchos anchos y de luz todos los baña
> Y a esos campos van los niños campesinos
> Sin un destino, sin un destino
> Son peregrinos de verdad."

I am certain of every lyric
as certain as I know my name.
Lula.   Lucrecia.   Light.

The words form images in my mind.
> I reach for them with my voice
> and sing.
> *I* sing.

> "The sun warms up wide ranches
> And bathes them all in light
> To those fields go the farmworker children
> Without a destiny, without a destiny
> True pilgrims in flight."

I am the only one singing now.

An orange-yellow wind swirls
from within me
      it flows out
            and into the air.
My whirring song comes from
      my lungs
      my throat
      my mouth
      my words,

      "¡Viva la huelga!
      ¡Viva la huelga!
      ¡Viva la causa de verdad!"

SET THE STAGE

Agustín, Luis, and
    the others cascade
        in applause and hoots!

"You have been hiding that beautiful voice from us this
whole time! You can probably act too!" Agustín says.

"So, do you think you can repeat this in public, right before El Teatro's performance?" Luis asks.

Like a ringmaster,
    this is my turn
        to set the stage
            for others!

"Yes, I can!" I say, nodding feverishly.

"Aja! That's the spirit! Si se puede, pequeña! ¡Sí se puede!"
Agustín says.

SEED SONG

Since the wind took my voice,
I feel whole again.

I am not windswept, nor robbed,
nor less of me.

The wind is my friend.
It helps carry my voice
no longer dusty and soft
but loud, silky, smooth
into the air.

But,
I am more than my voice.

I am a seed song.

Ready to share it with others,
ready to set it free.

ASLEEP, AGAIN

Mamá is like still water
when she sleeps.
She does so much of it lately.

> My mamá of yesterday
> was a frolicking river
> dancing along beds of growing kids,
> laboring in the fields while
> looking on the bright side of everything.

Her fight with the poison
shifts directions,
flowing in strength,
and sometimes
slowing with sleep.

> "Mamá, I want to tell you that I can sing," I whisper,
> hoping to wake her.

She doesn't hear me
not because of my voice,
because her water
is too still and too deep.

> I sit beside her and hum
> the movement's song.

CIRCUS HOUSE

Sometimes, our new house becomes
    a tiny circus where people meet
    after the meetings because
    we're so close to the union hall.

It gets wild with all us
    kids parading around plus
    anyone else's kids who come
    with their parents.

Paquita comes to help Mamá
    when Mamá has bad days and can't get up.
    Other times, because of the gas stove
    they cook and cook together
    with food donations from the alliance
    to help feed the strikers.

Tonight, Papá and Josesito
    come in late and sit down at the table.
    Paquita serves them the taquitos they made.
    Papá and Josesito glow when they tell us
    they'll be going on the march to Sacramento.

    "Cesar says this is a time for all farmworker Catholics
    to do penitence. To cleanse ourselves of all the bad
    we've done," Papá says while nodding.

Mamá slouches into her chair,
    though she claps at the news.
I am excited for Papá and Josesito.
I wish that I could go too
    but I don't dare ask.

PRACTICE MAKES PERFECT

The day of the meeting
>I practice the song I'll sing
>in the yard of our house
>>where I can see the Sierra
>>mountains leaning into the earth
>>like sleeping giants.

I belong on that pilgrimage
>with El Teatro, with Papá, and la causa.
>>Though Papá hasn't seen me sing yet,
>>I have to work up the nerve
>>to ask him if I can go.

Concha pushes through the
>screen door to find me in the yard.
>>Her eyes bloom
>>with amazement.

She shouts,

>"I got in! Lula! I got into San Jose State! With a full
>scholarship!" She jumps up and down.

Without a word,
>I rush her
>>and *I* lift her
>>with a gigantic hug!

We spin and spin.
>Our shrieks
>overflow with joy.

BREAKING

Rafa comes home with Martín
    asleep in his arms
        and Gabi toddling behind.

Mamá walks in by herself
    but drags her feet
        like a run-on sentence.

    "Doña Serafina and the nurses said she needs treatment
    in a hospital because they are limited with what they
    can do. She's got a referral to a specialist," he says as
    we watch Mamá drift off to sleep on the couch, holding
    a Virgen de Guadalupe prayer card in her hand.

We don't have
    money for a specialist.
We don't have
    money for a hospital.

This we know
    and it's terrifying.

Papá comes home then,
    looks puzzlingly at Mamá
    and at our faces sunken with susto.

As Rafa explains Mamá's situation
    Papá's face flushes red.

    "We have to do something about it as a family," Papá says.

    "Anything for Mamá," I say, and Rafa and Concha nod.

"We have to break the strike and get back to work on the fields." He pauses and we are stunned by what it will mean to stop supporting la causa. "I don't know what I was thinking agreeing to go on the march," he says.

We recover from the shock
    and fire away at him.

      "What? And lose everything we've struggled for?"
      Concha exclaims.

      "Your mother is more important than this or any move-
      ment!" Papá whips back.

Papá's worry for Mamá
    ignites the match of his temper,
but I stand up and calmly say,

      "Papá, be reasonable, Mamá is getting better. She just
      needs a little more help. Plus, tonight is the meeting to
      announce the march to Sacramento. You've got to go on
      the march."

      "I can't leave your mother like this!" he scolds me.

      "What if Concha and I go in your place?" I ask.

      "Have you lost your mind? Where is your loyalty to
      your family? We need all of our wages. Together we can
      make fifty dollars a day even working the dog wages
      the growers offer and not fifteen dollars a week like we
      are now."

      "Papá, our wins will be on the other side, that's what the

alliance says. Besides, something big is going to change, Cesar said so himself," Concha says.

"I am so tired of empty promises. It's been six months of no work. I'm tired of this strike, I'm tired of him, Larry Itliong, Dolores Huerta, and I'm tired of you all for believing them. No. More. I will not allow it any longer. We have to help your mother." Papá's voice trembles as if he is close to tears.

Something in Papá looks shattered.
He hunches his shoulders
and rubs his face.

"But we haven't even asked the alliance for help. If there is anyone who can find the resources to help us, it will be Dolores Huerta," Rafa says. "Plus, you don't need to stay. Go on the march, I can keep caring for Mamá."

"Papá, por favor. Let's just go to the meeting tonight," I plead.

"¡Está bien!" Papá lowers his head, stares hard at the floor, and breathes deeply. "Vamos, Rafa, you come with me to the meeting. Lula and Concha, you stay here."

When they leave,
            the ripped
            screen door
            slams
            like the
            meanest
            punctuation
            mark.

BLESSINGS

Mamá lies there
coming out of sleep
and witnessing it all
like a quiet brook.

She brings us close
assures us not to worry
she is going to get well.

> "Forgive your father," she says, "it scares him when I am
> sick. He's trying to do right, poco a poco." She reaches
> for our hands and squeezes firmly, and I trust that this
> strength will pull her through.

We tell Mamá about
Concha's acceptance
and my debut performance,
and she begins to cry
and quickly sits up to
cover us with her arms.

> "Mis hijas," she says, "my strong, smart, powerful girls. I
> am so proud of you. Vayan, go to the meeting. Go."

Though we are scared,
we set out for the meeting
to show Papá what Mamá can see in us
that he doesn't want to see.

Her hugs and her blessings
are the cool water we needed
to soothe Papá's burning words.

A PERCH

We scan the packed room for Papá.
I see Rafa first. He's found Dolores Huerta!

   He walks away from Dolores
   with a huge smile swinging on his face
   and he heads right for us.

        But someone calls my name. "Lula!"
        I turn to see Agustín
        holding his guitar and waving me over.

            Concha gives me a soft push
            as if sending a paper boat into a stream.

                I give Concha and Rafa a thumbs-up
                as I walk away and take my place
                near the stairs of the stage with El Teatro.

   From that small perch
        Rafa and Concha approach Papá.
        Rafa points at Dolores and smiles.
        I know she's agreed to help Mamá!

        Then, I see Concha give Papá
        her acceptance letter.

                Papá's face moves like wind
                from wicked and harsh to subtle and soft.
                I catch its sway when Papá
                        sees me take the stage.

BEFORE I SING

I don't feel scared
of Papá, or the growers,
the police, or the scabs.

I *believe* in our causa
and my role in it.

I push through the earth

    a girl, sprouting,

    smart, growing, budding

    powerful, extending, flowering

        with an orange-yellow voice, returned

        no longer a seed but a sunflower

        holding many other seeds in me and our
        movement

        reaching high above the ground

        to touch the sun.

TWISTED PAPÁ

Papá rushes through the crowd
up to the stage, his chest rising
and falling with his breath.

I sing into the microphone
        and look into his eyes.

        Fully me. Whole. Completa.

When he gets near me,
        Papá's face is
                twisted in sadness.
Or is it happiness?

                He gets closer and
        it becomes clear
Papá is crying.

He blinks away the rain in his eyes
        when a smile breaks the clouds
                and it appears on his face like a bright sky.

                His smile, missing its right-side molar,
        is because of me and for me!

When I bow,
        I hear his applause.
                I hear his pride in me.
                        When I come up,
        I rise with my own applause.
I am proud of me.

BRAZOS ABIERTOS

I run off stage and into
     Papá's wide-open arms that don't speak
         but say, "I'm sorry."
         Though it means more
         when I hear him say,

    "I'm sorry for being so hard on you, Lula. And you, Concha, and Rafa. For not believing in what you can do. I had no idea. I was so wrong."

Our tears curve down
     our cheeks,
         Rafa's, Concha's, mine.

Papá touches our faces
with his calloused hands
one by one,
     peeling away
         the hurt he's caused,
         with a true apology
         from deep in his heart
         and with the words.

    "I love you, mis hijos. Los quiero tanto."

Just then,
     Dolores Huerta takes the stage.

Papá drapes one arm over me
     and another over Concha
and I slide my free arm around Rafa.

We take slower breaths,
    nodding our heads,
as we listen to her speech
    move through us and ground us.
Feeling connected
    to one another
and to our purpose
        to carry on.

DOLORES SPEAKS

"Brothers and sisters,   tomorrow   we march to Sacramento.
We are going to call   every farmworker   in every field we pass,
every supporter in   every city   we pass to come join us
in finding equality for   the farm   workers who help feed
the nation. We will march right up to Governor Brown's office in
Sacramento to let him know that we mean business. We are
citizens and residents of the state of California and we won't
stop until there are fair wages and fair treatments in the
fields. We'll let the governor and the legislature of California know they can't close their eyes and their
ears to us any longer. They can't pretend
we don't exist. They can't plead ignorance
to our problems because we are here,
we embody the needs of all workers.
We are on the rise.
In Delano, we've
shown what can
be done. And
we must show
them that we are not alone. There are men, women, and children
from across the country demanding equality. The day has ended
when the farmworker will let himself be used as a pawn by employers,
government, and others who would exploit him for their own
ends. La huelga and la causa is our cry, and everyone must listen.
¡Viva la huelga! ¡Viva la causa!"

PACKING LOVE

When we get home,
a sweetness
hovers above us.

The babies are asleep.
Mamá is up and packing
not one small satchel, but three.

Wrapped ham tortas, fruit, jars with water.

　　"Who are they for, Mamá?" Concha asks.

　　"For Papá, you, and Lula." Her smile flashes us with light.

Papá agrees with Mamá
with a delicate wink.

Without even being there,
Mamá trusted Papá
would come around
when he saw for himself
what we had to give.

Rafa almost tackles us
as we huddle and jump,
bursting with happiness!

　　"These children of ours, Mamá, have really blown me
　　away. They are more powerful than I ever knew." Papá
　　combs down my hair and looks right at me. "Did you
　　know Lula can sing like a cenzontle?"

"Sí, viejo." Mamá nods, still smiling. "They have always been that special! I am so happy you finally understand."

My family folds
into a rose of hugs,
but this time
it includes Papá,
like a petal
woven in.

Delano, California • March 1966

MARCH

We step out into the morning,
Delano dawn being born
into a new day.

The march to Sacramento.
340 miles.
75 farmworkers.
El Teatro Campesino.
Our banner, La Virgen de Guadalupe.
A pilgrimage.
A statement.
A seed bundle of hope.

Papá, Concha, and me
kiss
Mamá, Rafa, Gabi, and Martín
goodbye
with short little kisses
and a bendición drawn in the air
by Mamá's gentle gestures.

     I take Papá's hand
and he takes
     Concha's hand.
We join the crowd in singing,,

     "De colores, de colores se visten los campos en la
     primavera . . ."

We march for justice, together.

¡SÍ SE PUEDE!

—Dolores Huerta

Dear Reader,

Thank you for taking this journey into the seed cycle of Lula's story, into a not-too-distant past, to a place and people so essential to our country's survival: the farmlands and the farmworkers of California and the United States. Sadly, the struggle for fair pay and just working conditions is still being fought. In many instances, conditions for farmworkers are the same today as they were in 1965. The farming industry continues to exploit workers across the country by using harmful pesticides without protections, paying low wages, providing very poor housing, and so on. Women and children are burdened by many more of these abuses because of their gender and age. United States child labor laws (which protect children from exploitation) don't apply to farmwork—the only industry in the nation that does not abide by them. Many children continue to work the fields alongside their parents or as migrant unaccompanied minors today. I wrote Lula's story, at the invitation of my editor, Nancy Mercado, as a way to honor farmworkers and the beginnings of one of the greatest labor justice movements undertaken in United States history.

History belongs to those who write it or those who tell it. With the 1960s came a deep awakening to injustice and the beginning of significant efforts to build a more just world across the globe, but particularly in the United States. The fight for civil rights for ethnic and racial minorities and women emerged alongside the fight for worker's rights and economic rights. When researching this project, I sought out dozens of books and accounts about the first moments of the 1965 Delano grape strike, which include many versions, testimonies, and descriptions of the same events. I did, however, learn some significant facts that have been written out of or buried in this particular history. For instance, while much of the credit for the beginning of the movement has been given to Mexican organizers and workers, it was Filipino workers led by Larry Itliong and Philip Veracruz of the Agricultural Workers Organizing Committee who courageously began the Delano grape strike. Dolores Huerta and Cesar Chávez and their National Farm Workers Association joined the strike two weeks after. It was a coalition of multi-ethnic and multi-racial workers that went on strike together and would eventually become the United Farm Workers—a union that remains active today.

Another important fact I learned is that women and children were at the center of many of the organizing efforts, yet not many were given leadership positions, with the exceptions of Dolores Huerta and Helen Chávez. And still, Dolores Huerta's powerful contributions as lead negotiator were hardly documented during those first days. Women's and children's voices are largely missing in many historical records, and I had to dig deep to find their accounts. I was lucky enough to interview my friends Ismael, Reynalda, and María Rodríguez, who were children and teen migrant farmworkers in 1965 in California (and who grew up to work as organizers for the UFW) to uncover many of the details I needed to build Lula's world.

I also drew upon the many stories told to me by my mother about when she was a migrant farmworking child, the daughter of a bracero (contracted seasonal workers from Mexico who first came to the United States to help labor shortages during WWII). My abuelito, Jose Maria Viramontes, who was a loving and caring man, came to the United States with his family to work the harvests during the 1950s. While braceros were some of the laborers who crossed the picket line during this struggle in 1965, my abuelito's tenure as a bracero ended before this strike. In 1955, he was paralyzed from the waist down when the bed of the truck on which he was riding on the way out to work the fields unhinged, and he was thrown off the truck and broke his back. He was sent back to Mexico with a disability pension so insignificant that he and our family lived out the rest of his days in deep poverty. I tried to honor my family's work and legacy, and to reflect some of the exploitation they experienced, in these pages.

While we have made huge strides in the feminist and women's movements, true equity for girls and women is still very much needed. There are fathers, brothers, bosses, and men in positions of power who continue to deny women the rights to safety from physical abuse and to our due respect in the home, in leadership roles, and in any workplace or industry. I strove to provide a look inside this time of political upheaval and mass change from the lens of one girl who found a way to speak up and fight against oppressive sexist conditions. We must not give up fighting to right these wrongs because we all win, now and in future generations, when we can lift one another.

A note about language. Because this story takes place in 1965, there are words used for people of different racial groups both in descriptive and negative ways. For instance, Black people were referred to as "Negro" at the time. Though today this term is not often used, it was what Black people called themselves and it was considered an improvement on the N word, which came out of the horrors of slavery. It wasn't until 1966 that the Black Panther Party made the term *Black* a beautiful word filled with self-love and community power. *Oakie* was used to describe, without much prejudice, white migrant farmworkers who came to California from Oklahoma during the Dust Bowl of the 1930s.

Similarly, *Manong* is a word used by Filipinos to self-identify with their cultural heritage. The words *Flip* and *Spik*, which are short versions of *Filipino* and *Spanish-speaking*, were derogatory then and continue to be. The word *scab* was also a negative word used against strike breakers. Some of these words created many divisions that were counter to the calls for civil rights being raised. I chose to use them in dialogue to reflect the times and the characters who used them. However, in all honesty, it is difficult to use them at *any* time because they are hurtful.

I believe the arts are a way to bring about profound social justice and personal transformation. It is the reason why I write. Dolores Huerta has called El Teatro Campesino one of the most powerful organizing tools the UFW had during that time. El Teatro Campesino used theater and the arts to help the farmworker struggle by performing political theater (theater with a message) on the backs of the bed of trucks and anywhere the farmworkers gathered. Their work sparked a long-lasting Chicane theater movement and inspired many performers and troupes to use the arts to heal and to stand up to injustice the world over.

You will find real-life historical figures like Dolores Huerta, Helen and Cesar Chávez, Larry Itliong, Gil Padilla, Esther Urunday, Luis Valdez, and Agustín Lira highlighted in this story. Because this is a work of historical fiction, what they do and say in the book is taken directly from some of their speeches or actos I found during my research, or were fictionalized versions of moments of iconic photos or footage of their work. We must always consider that there is always more to any person's story so we don't put anyone on an untouchable pedestal. I chose to feature these labor and arts leaders so that we can honor the larger impact some of their choices and efforts made on the movement for labor rights, for the arts, and in many people's lives.

Ultimately, Lula's story is only a seed, as are you. It is an invitation for you to plant what you've learned in the garden of your heart and mind, to dig and till for more facts and history, to cultivate it with time and patience by thinking deeper about the role of farmworkers in our every meal. It is an invitation to harvest it with more understanding, compassion, and appreciation for their struggle. So that ultimately, it will bloom and you too are compelled to support farmworkers and their fight for justice through your voice, through your art making, or in any way you think is right.

Always remember: that which is planted—when given the right conditions, attention, and love—will grow.

Con amor,
Aida

Want to learn more about the Delano Grape Strike, the UFW, or the Labor Movement of the 1960s? Here are some of the books and websites I pored over while doing research for this book.

NON-FICTION BOOKS FOR YOUNGER READERS

Dolores Huerta: Get to Know the Voice of Migrant Workers by Robert Liu-Trujillo

Side by Side: The Story of Dolores Huerta and Cesar Chávez by Monica Brown, illustrated by Joe Cepeda

Journey for Justice: The Life of Larry Itliong by Dawn B. Mabalon, PhD, and Gayle Romansanta, illustrated by Andre Sibayan

The Circuit: Stories from the Life of a Migrant Child by Francisco Jiménez

Breaking Through by Francisco Jiménez

NON-FICTION BOOKS FOR OLDER READERS

A Dolores Huerta Reader, edited by Mario T. Garcia

Puro Teatro: A Latina Anthology, edited by Alberto Sandoval-Sánchez and Nancy Saporta Sternbach. Testimony: "Searching for Sanctuaries: Cruising through Town in a Red Convertible" by Diane Rodríguez

El Teatro Campesino: Theater in the Chicano Movement by Yolanda Broyles-González

Chasing the Harvest: Migrant Workers in California Agriculture, edited by Gabriel Thomas

Huelga: The First Hundred Days of the Great Delano Grape Strike by Eugene Nelson

DOCUMENTARIES / FILMS / VIDEOS

Dolores, directed by Peter Bratt for PBS

Harvest of Shame, directed by Edward R. Murrow

The Delano Manongs, directed by Marissa Aroy

Adios Amor, directed by Laurie Coyle

Cesar Chávez (biopic), directed by Diego Luna

Chicano! History of the Mexican-American Civil Rights Movement, part two, "The Struggle in the Fields"

Dolores Huerta on El Teatro Campesino:
www.youtube.com/watch?v=D0AMyilwIfo

Luis Valdez Beginnings:
https://www.youtube.com/watch?v=8qWNjXjHxo8

PHOTO ARCHIVES

Paul Richards Photo Archive 1955–1966 at Estuary Press

Bob Fitch Farmworker Photo Archive at Stanford University

Jon Lewis Photo Archive at Yale University

Walter P. Reuther Library at Wayne State University

Claudio Beagarie Archive at Boise State University

WEBSITES

Farmworker Movement Documentation Project
(includes oral histories, videos, and photos) at UC San Diego:
https://libraries.ucsd.edu/farmworkermovement/

UFW: www.UFW.org

Dolores Huerta Foundation: www.DoloresHuerta.org

El Teatro Campesino: www.ElTeatroCampesino.com

El Teatro Campesino Archives at UCSB

National Center for Farmworker Health: www.ncfh.org

National Farmworker Ministry: www.nfwm.org

Filipino American National Historical Society:
http://fanhs-national.org/filam/

ACKNOWLEDGMENTS

I owe my deepest gratitude to a wide bounty of people who helped make *A Seed in the Sun* possible.

To my extraordinary editor, Nancy Mercado, gracias infinitas for planting the first seed. It is because of your vision and your invitation that I was able to make this new contribution to middle grade literature about this movement. Your gentle patience and sharp insights helped me cultivate a story both true to me and to history that I hope will also reach readers' hearts. Thank you also to Rosie Ahmed for your phenomenal editorial support and for helping me find the right words to honor all people. Muchísimas gracias to Marietta Zacker, who is part agent and part wonder woman and always my rock. Thank you to the team at Dial Books and Penguin who've done so much to make me feel welcome in my new home—Carmela Iaria, Venessa Carson, Summer Ogata, Trevor Ingerson, Judith Huerta, Jordana Kulak, Oliva Russo. To copy editors Regina Castillo and Ariela Rudy Zaltzman, thank you for your eagle eyes. Much, much gratitude to cover illustrator Karina Perez, and cover designer Jess Jenkins, as well as book designer Jason Henry, for making this book so gorgeous! Gracias de todo corazón to accuracy readers and historical sources, some of whom are my dearest friends, Akira Boch, Maria Elena Fernandez (bff adorada), Gilbert Padilla, Reinalda Nuñez-Rodriguez, Ismael Rodriguez, Maria Rodriguez, and Gayle Romasanta. Your lived experiences and historical and artistic expertise helped bring nuance and honesty to this story in such rich ways and I am so grateful. Thank you to a fantastic ecosystem of writers, librarians, teachers, and readers too many to name, who have extended their amazing support. I promise to hug you when I finally get to see you.

To Dolores Huerta, Helen Chávez, Esther Urunday, Maria Moreno, Virginia Rodriguez, Lorraine Agtang, Lupe Valdez, Diane Rodriguez, and to all women activists and artists both living and gone, known and unknown, your indispensable contributions to the farmworker movement will live on. Thank you for your sacrifices and for your tenacious work for justice.

Gracias del alma to my mami and sister both now ancestors, Maria Isabel Viramontes and Isabel Salazar, whose indelible imprints are delicately cast throughout this story. And to my maternal grandfather, Jose Maria Viramontes, my father, Fidel Rafael Salazar, and my brother, Rafael Salazar, thank you for challenging and redefining what it means to be a tender and brave man in my life.

To my corazones, John, Avelina, and Joao Santos, my teachers and my sustenance. Your love is the seed that makes me grow and flourish. Gracias, mis amores.